12days Of Christr

12 Days Of Christmas: 2017

Compiled

By

Matthew Cash and Em Dehaney

BURDIZZO BOOKS 2017

12days Of Christmas:2017

Copyright Matthew Cash Burdizzo Books 2017

Edited by Matthew Cash, Burdizzo Books

All rights reserved. No part of this book may be reproduced in any form or by any means, except by inclusion of brief quotations in a review, without permission in writing from the publisher. Each author retains copyright of their own individual story.

This book is a work of fiction. The characters and situations in this book are imaginary. No resemblance is intended between these characters and any persons, living, dead, or undead.

This book is sold subject to the condition that it shall not, by way of trade or otherwise, be lent, resold, hired out or otherwise circulated without the publisher's prior consent in any form or binding or cover other than that in which it is published and without similar condition including this condition being imposed on the subsequent purchaser

Published in Great Britain in 2017 by Matthew Cash, Burdizzo Books, Walsall, UK

Contents

12. Drummers Drumming ....
David Court..5

11. Pipers Piping ....
Matthew Cash...49

10. Lords Leaping..
Mark Nye...65

9. Ladies Dancing..
Pippa Bailey..83

8. Maids Milking..
Dani Brown..117

7. Swans A Swimming..................................
G. H. Finn 145

6. Geese Laying..
Mark Leney..163

5. Gold Rings..

Em Dehaney 179

4. Calling Birds ....

Anthony Cowin 185

3. French Hens ....

Peter Germany 209

2. Turtle Doves ....

Richard Wall 225

A Partridge In A Pear Tree ....

Lex H Jones 249

Bonus Material 275

The Incredible True Story of Red Sleigh Down (Santa's Stripy 'Oss] ....

Ian Henery 277

Author Biographies 285

12. Drummers Drumming
David Court

Not only am I too late, but they'd had time to go to work on him.

Solomon's wracked corpse has clearly been left for me to find, hanging from a crooked lamppost with tinsel-wrapped rope, a gruesome display of both gaud and gore. I shimmy up the pole to cut him loose, and his body falls to the cracked tarmac with an organic thud.

A casual onlooker might consider my actions merciful, as though I were planning on giving my old companion a more dignified resting place than the one those monsters gave him – my reasons are, however, altogether less than altruistic.

It's not the first time I've done this. Solomon's ruined face is a bloodied labyrinth of scars and incisions. Sometimes it's easier when they take the eyes so you don't have them staring at you.

I begin to prise open his jaw, but from the feel of his gums through his skin I suspect I'm wasting my time. His mouth is empty and filled with blood, a leaking scarlet maw of crudely mauled tissue.

They've taken his teeth already. I'll have no luck there. I'll just have to hope that the meagre collection of molars and canines I've already amassed will be enough to barter my way through The Dives.

I sense the shift in the air moments before my Pigeon band starts to vibrate against my wrist. I jumped to my feet and spin around just in time to see him bearing down on me, his pace slowing from a sprint to a jog. Despite the madness wrapping its tendrils around his addled brain, there's still some reasoning there. Now he knows I'm aware of his presence, there's a certain reticence. He's weighing me up, considering his options.

Even at their most intelligent though, they're far from sophisticated creatures. His options consist of fighting or fleeing, and it's rare that a Drummer will choose the latter. Especially as, in this case, he must consider himself the superior combatant. I'm a female (easily a head shorter than him) and appear unarmed.

He's dragging an old rusted rake with a bent metal handle. As he raises it aloft, his mouth opens wide in a silent scream, spittle spraying out from his slathering jaws. Even when I pull out my blade – a vicious serrated thing – he barely slows.

We circle, staring each other down. His mouth is moving, his lips twisting into barked words. He's trying to intimidate me, forgetting – or oblivious to the fact –

that I can't hear him. Still, it's having its intended purpose. I can lip-read the odd word and none of them are pleasant. It's clear that he wants to either rape me or disfigure me, and he's not fussed about which order he does it in.

His ears are a blotched mess of tumours and inflamed growths. It's been a while since I've seen one this far along the infection lifecycle that could still operate semi-intelligently. By this stage they're usually vicious, subhuman creatures driven solely by instinct, past the point of using tools or weaponry.

It's only when the rusted spikes of the rake miss my head by inches that I realise I'm allowing myself to become distracted again. Regardless of how infected they are, it's idiocy to ever consider them anything less than a genuine threat.

Holding the handle of the rake in both hands, he swings it around in a vicious arc, and it's only by throwing myself to the ground that I avoid being hit. I jab upwards with the knife in the moments that he's recovering his balance, the blade sliding neatly into his left thigh. I'm rewarded with a torrent of blood spilling out over his tattered clothes, and he staggers backwards. With luck, I've hit his femoral artery, and he'll bleed out in minutes.

Another swipe from the rake, but one-handed this time and more desperate than the last. I throw myself at him – even with my comparatively small frame, the injury to his leg causes him to lose his footing and he falls backwards.

I don't give him the opportunity to get back up. By the time his flailing hands are at my throat, I've stabbed him a good half a dozen times about the neck, slicing through both his jugular and carotid arteries. He lurches up at the last moment to bite at me, and the last slice ends up severing one of the tumorous patches from the side of his head. It falls away, like a huge bloodied scab.

He dies twitching just as the odour hits me – it smells of rancid food left to rot, and the aroma is still something I'll never get used to. It's all I can do to stop myself from retching as I open the thing's mouth to stare despondently at a mouthful of worn out, worthless, diseased teeth and blackened gums. A gasp of foul air belches out of the thing as I push the corpse away.

An unkempt garden from a nearby house serves as the final resting place for Solomon. I've heard rumours that some of the bands of Drummers have taken to cannibalism, and the poor guy has suffered enough. The cold winter earth is tough and unforgiving, and its growing dark when I've finished the job and patted the ground flat. The house will have to serve as my shelter for the evening.

When I've finally attached Pigeon sensors to all the ways into the building, I realise my stock of masking tape is dwindling fast and I'm forced to be sparing with the last couple, hoping they'll remain attached overnight. I do one last recce of the house and check that each of the sensors is synched to the band I wear, tiny green lights on the surface of the sensors matching the heartbeat of the thing that pulses against my wrist.

I prop myself in a corner behind the door in an upstairs room, my knife at hand. It's as I'm sitting there in the twilight, mulling over the events of the day, when I see it. Strands of red and green tinsel are clinging to my filthy cargo trousers, sparkling pieces of foil glittering in the fading light. It seemed remarkably cruel, yet novel, for the Drummers to present Solomon as such a festive trophy. I was sure it was December, but was it nearly Christmas? Had Christmas come and gone? Such traditions seemed frivolous now, a thing confined to history.

No, not ancient history – just a single year.

One single Christmas ago, the day when all the noises stopped. How terrifying it must have been in those initial few hours when the true horror dawned – when individuals who'd found themselves suddenly deaf realised that everybody else had been similarly affected.

You know that expression, "In the kingdom of the blind, the one-eyed man is king?" Until that day, I'd never really contemplated its full meaning. I, however, had an advantage over all of those affected on that fateful day.

I was born deaf. I'd never known anything else. As society struggled, I was forced to lead, to teach.

Life staggered on, as normal as it could. The phenomenon was worldwide, and whereas science discovered a cause, it couldn't discover a reason. They nicknamed it Shrike, and it was a condition affecting the eardrums of every hearing human on the planet.

At that stage, it looked like society might adapt - but then things got much worse. Some of those affected, in increasing numbers, began to report their hearing returning. Some optimistically began to believe that all would similarly recover, but then those supposed lucky few began to hear other sounds – the sound of distant rhythmic drumming.

The drumming sound grew louder with each passing hour, ceaseless and maddening. Even in sleep, the rhythmic beats persisted, and those affected quickly went insane.

Drummers, the press called them. Angry, violent, and slowly becoming the majority. Physical signs began to mark them out – the infection that affected the eardrum became visible, tumours and lesions forming around the ear canal. Drummers would also jerk violently like yanked marionettes, each spasm accompanying the staccato rhythm that only they could hear inside their minds.

Society collapsed in weeks. Outnumbered by an enemy that they couldn't hear, mankind hid. The Powers That Be vanished, either killed or cowering underground like rats.

In my dreams, I feel the beat of the drums. In my subconscious though, I know I'm safe – for the time being. My restless mind is just interpreting the rhythmic pulse of the Pigeon band on my wrist.

The Pigeon band is a bit of jury-rigged, now commonplace technology – it hears for you. Noises, dependent on the volume and duration, register as anything from vibrations of varying strengths to small electric shocks through the band. The sensors I've dotted around are merely remote extensions of the same technology, relaying noises back to the receiver.

Simple, easy and cheap to manufacture, and critical to survival. Having been deaf for all my life, nearly forty years has seen my other senses improve to compensate and I'm trying not to rely on the band, but it's very easy to slip into habit.

A sharp jolt wakes me from my half-sleep, letting me know that one of the sensors against a window has been triggered. I've trained myself enough that I'm wide awake in seconds, my hand around the hilt of the knife.

The Drummers tend to have a tell-tale smell, the reek of the infection lingering in the air around them – the acrid aroma of decay. There's none of that, only the faint trace of sulphur in the air, which in my experience, is typically associated with guns and cheap ammunition.

The door to my room slowly opens and I stay put in my corner, watching the long-barrel silencer tip of a revolver emerge into the room. A survivor then, but I'm just as likely to meet my end from a panicked shot if I startle them. For a moment, it looks as though the weapon's wielder isn't going to approach any further, but then they suddenly step inside, gun focused at the room's empty far corner.

I put my hands in the air just as the intruder trains their gun upon me. Even though my actions confirm I'm not a Drummer, they don't relax quite yet. There are plenty of survivors out there in the wildlands who are only looking out for themselves. You can't trust anybody.

I know the drill – I'm not stupid enough to think I stand a chance against a loaded pistol. The knife falls from my grip and I feel the thud as it lands on the wooden floor beside me. With a push, I slide the knife across the floor where it lands against their thick leather boot. Without taking their eyes off me, the intruder crouches down and picks it up. They've done this before – the pistol remains trained on my body, not on my head. It presents a larger target and one that they'll have plenty of opportunity to shoot should I lunge at them. Chest or belly, even a glancing blow, I'm as good as dead out here without medical aid.

They point up with fingerless gloved hands, clearly indicating for me to stand. In the dim light, they're nothing more than a silhouette and I think they're deliberately exaggerating their signing so I can see it in the darkness.

Alright, I nod and sign back with two thumbs up, sliding my back up against the wall.

Who are you? The pistol is slightly lowered now, but not enough that I dare make a move.

I fingerspell Melody, deliberately taking my time.

Paxton, they sign back. I have no idea whether that's a surname, or a boy or girl's forename. From the physique and build, I'm pretty sure it's a man I'm dealing with. It's followed by more signing, still slow and deliberate. I'm now concluding that their hesitance is due to their relative inexperience with signing and not that they're being slow on my account. I've taught enough signing (it's an invaluable skill now, and we're highly revered) to know a person's proficiency with it.

Why are you here?

I match their speed in my reply. I don't want to either confuse or intimidate them.

It got dark. Sheltering.

Where are you from?

Birmingham.

There's a slump in the silhouette's shoulders as they relax slightly. The lowering of tension in the room is almost palpable, and the gun lowers slightly as they step forward. He's a white male, well-built with a crewcut which looks self-administered. He's more boy than man though, another teen hurriedly recruited into a desperate army. I've been around enough military to recognise the type. He begins signing a reply, but a sudden jolt of electricity surges through my wrist.

I interrupt him and hurriedly sign directly in front of his face.

Alone?

He nods, a confused expression forming across his face. I point to the plastic band on my wrist and he seems to understand. They're a universal piece of kit these days, instantly recognisable. Far too trusting, he moves alongside me, both of us hiding in the shadows behind the door.

If I were a scavenger, this'd be the point where I slid the blade into one of his vital organs, having faked the Pigeon alarm. Luckily for him, I'm not.

This time, I can smell the Drummer drawing nearer, like something from Satan's own arse-crack. A foulness that reeks of long decaying meat, cloying at the back of my throat and causing us both to dry heave. I can feel the gentle vibrations in the walls as it thuds into them through its haphazard stumbles across the landing.

Truth is, we don't know how they hunt. Some of them are plain stupid, barely capable of registering something right in front of their face. Others seem to have an unerring habit of tracking their victims. The terrifying thing is that there's no pattern.

The Drummer staggers into our room and towards the broken window, a shaft of dull moonlight reflecting across his warped features. This one is pretty far gone, his ears reduced to tiny sphincter-like holes amongst a mass of blistered tissue on each side of his ravaged face. We haven't been spotted. Yet.

Shoot, I sign, agitated. Paxton brushes me away, brow furrowed. I sign it again, my gestures more exaggerated this time, registering my annoyance. Before I can insist for a third time, he's taken his own blade out and is creeping up behind the Drummer.

The Drummer is standing perfectly still, staring captivated at a perfect full moon that hangs outside. His head is swaying gently left to right, as though he's hypnotised by the fluorescent lunar orb. The light glints against Paxton's wicked looking blade.

The Drummer, suddenly roused to our presence, spins around. A flailing arm strikes Paxton, who's caught unawares and sent staggering backwards. The blade bounces noiselessly off the floor and lands by the filthy rat-holed skirting board. The Drummer's beady black eyes look from Paxton to me, and then back to Paxton again.

The Drummer throws himself at the poor soldier before he can lunge for his blade. He's straddling the boy, raining blows down upon him. Holding my knife, I run over to them and yank back on the hood of the Drummer's jacket. I'm hoping to pull his head back so I can slide the blade into his throat, but he takes me by surprise when he gets to his feet and arms raised, turns to face me.

He grabs at me and I'm sent floundering backwards, with insufficient distance between us for me to get a decent stab in. He stops in the centre of the room just as an unsteady Paxton is getting back up to his feet, his eyes darting between the two of us as he considers which will be the easier target.

Shoot! I gesture.

The Drummer, to my astonishment, looks back towards the blade and, rather than take either of us on unarmed, staggers towards the window. I've never seen this level of reasoning from one so infected.

I'm not going to let him surprise me again and I lunge at him. The window frame is a muddle of wooden splinters with no glass, and my plan is to push him out of it and break the creature's neck with the fall.

This day is ending up full of surprises.

The Drummer grabs at me and my momentum carries us both out of the window. A desperate outstretched hand at the frame comes too late, and I close my eyes tightly shut as we plummet towards the hard earth outside.

I open my eyes to find myself lying on the wheezing and trembling body of the Drummer, who ended up cushioning my fall. I clamber to my feet but it doesn't make any attempt to do the same.

I think I've broken it.

Paxton appears in the doorway, a little bruised and bloodied from the brief skirmish – and perhaps just a little humbled – but okay. I slide the tip of the blade in through the back of the things neck, and it falls still.

Why didn't you just shoot him? I sign.

I ran out of ammo back at Croydon, he replies, sheepishly.

Luckily, our relieved laughter doesn't disturb any Drummers hiding in the dark.

We take it in turns to watch over the other, each of us getting some well-needed sleep. There's already enough trust between the two of us for that – formal introductions can wait.

My dreams are mostly abstract; fleeting images of Solomon, both alive and dead. In a few snapshots of our overlapping lives he's happy – in the majority, though, he's frustrated, anxious to move on from the temporary shelter we've found ourselves in. The mission, he keeps signing as a reminder, the mission. I can see his hands focus on the words, each in crystal clear definition – the whorls on his fingers, the pores on his skin, the callouses on his knuckles.

The sun was partly risen when Paxton woke me. I gave you an extra hour, he signed, you looked peaceful. On his turn, the boy sleeps like a corpse, arms and legs perfectly straight, his chest barely moving.

We eat a meagre breakfast, sharing elements of each other's for variety. A sachet of apple & cinnamon muesli from his day rations, a few oatmeal biscuits from my rucksack. Some bottled water added to his powdered chocolate milkshake is drinkable if not particularly pleasant.

I do the necessary step of breaking the ice.

Why are you alone?

Separated from my squadron.

What happened to them?

He pauses. I don't know if he's hesitating because he's struggling to remember the appropriate signing, or whether he's reluctant to tell me.

Don't know.

Where are you going now? I ask, secretly hoping he's going my way. I'd expected to have caught up with Solomon at this stage and to be travelling with him, but... best laid plans. It's always better to travel in numbers – the increased risk of being discovered is easily outweighed by the advantages of greater manpower. The ability to have a good night's sleep, for one.

Catterick Garrison, he fingerspells. That's good – I'm heading up to the Pennines, and with a minor detour, that's on the way. I sign as such, and he smiles. It looks like I have a travelling companion. One that won't be quite as good at philosophical discussions as poor Solomon, but he'll do.

My motives for delivering the boy to his Garrison are not entirely philanthropic. I know that a few of my colleagues – before we lost contact - were due to establish a research base somewhere in North Yorkshire to research the Shrike, and it's entirely possible that they've set up there.

The boy and I travel off-road, keeping away from the towns and cities. The Drummers tend not to roam far, so population centres are best avoided. The ones in the wilds tend to congregate in smaller numbers, so present less of a threat.

There's a stroke of luck on the second day when we come across a delivery van at the edge of a farmer's field. Looks like the driver, of whom there is no sign, tried to take the vehicle off-road and quickly found that it wasn't designed for rough terrain. It's from a local snack manufacturer – Boarwell's – and the back of the van is laden with hundreds of bags of Pork Scratchings. We cheerfully grab all that our rucksack and backpacks will allow.

At times, Paxton seems a million miles away. He'll communicate, but only when prompted. It takes the best part of a day to find out that he was recruited with very little training and left out of his depth with an equally unskilled squadron. Oddly, not once does the boy ask me why I'm travelling to the Pennines. Either he's afraid to ask, or he simply doesn't care. Nor does he seem to want to talk about the circumstances in which he ended up alone. I don't press him.

Even from our distant vantage point on a nearby hilltop, it's clear that Catterick has been abandoned. I go to comfort Paxton, but think better of it when it's clear that he looks unaffected, as though he'd prepared himself for exactly this outcome. The vehicles from the motor pool have all gone, the deep tracks of tanks and armoured cars snaking randomly across the fields surrounding the base.

The outside of the base is, luckily, deserted. He follows me down towards the gates like a lost puppy. The first thing that strikes me as I walk between the huge metal doors and stare into the courtyard is that there are no bodies. I've seen bases fall in Molesworth, Invicta, Camberwell, and this isn't like any of those.

Looks like everybody just upped and left.

With the boy following silently, I walk through a succession of abandoned rooms. Nothing has been taken, and nothing is in disarray. The offices and some of the barracks are even decorated for Christmas, brightly coloured tinsel and garlands garishly dangling from plain walls.

The boy's mood doesn't even improve when we come across the fully laden armoury, its inventory barely touched. Without emotion, he selects an Assault Rifle and bundles enough ammunition to start a small war into his rucksack. I'm not keen on guns but, not wishing to look a gift horse in the mouth, pick up a Glock 17 pistol and ammunition.

It's when we're scouring through the few remaining rooms in the base – confident enough to do so alone now – that he comes bounding into the locker room I'm exploring, looking more enthused than he has since we first arrived.

I've found something, he signs, hurriedly. Without pause, he's off.

He's standing outside the door to a room when I reach the corridor, gesturing at the contents.

I saw from the markings on your backpack that you're a scientist, he signs, and this looks like it'll interest you.

I'd forgotten the Science Division logo and serial number on my backpack. Goes some way to explaining why he didn't ask who I was. Perhaps he's sharper than I suspected.

The room looks like it was a library before it was made into a makeshift lab. Bookcases and their contents – books spanning the decades – have all been pushed into one corner to make room. Understandably, literature wasn't on the priority list after the apocalypse.

Two improvised workbenches hold a variety of pieces of equipment. A centrifuge, a bulky ruggedised laptop, and two portable refrigerator units are powered up, the emergency generator of the base still providing enough juice to keep them going.

It's then I spy the cup perched on the edge of one of the tables, fractal growths of mould emerging from within to creep over the vessel's lip. I recognise it as a retirement present we'd got for Alice, the boss of our lab. We'd had it custom printed especially for her, finding it difficult to find any matching the unique theme we were going for. It was plain white, bearing the legend "Environmental toxicologists do it quietly". She'd planned to retire at the end of the year, but the Shrike had put paid to that.

So, we'd missed each other. The old department password still worked on her laptop though, so I could at least try to find out what she'd been working on. And what had happened to her.

Alice never was the most organized in our department, and her desktop was covered with folders and documents of countless formats. This would take some time.

Paxton is hanging around in the room like an eager child, peering at everything I can see.

I grab his attention.

Shall we stay here until tomorrow? I ask. There are a lot of notes to go through.

He shrugs.

Is it okay if I have a look around? He asks, as though he needs permission. I nod and he slopes off.

It's a dull and laborious job, but by trawling through file dates, I manage to piece together a chronology of her notes. It looks like our studies into the Shrike overlapped for a while but then – apparently at the behest of the military staff gracious and patient enough to house Alice and her team – they began to concentrate on finding a cure.

Despite her lackadaisical approach to computer housekeeping, Alice was a stickler for laboratory guidelines. It's clear from the timings that her team rushed or were pressured into getting results, with all clinical standards loosened or, in some cases, bypassed completely. Despite the first cure prototype not working on the Drummer they'd captured, they continued with human trials regardless.

Alice and her team, reluctantly, at first, followed by a handful of soldiers ordered to do so. And then everybody.

And what's more, it appeared to work. Damaged eardrums began to heal, and the experiment was deemed a complete success. I stared at the words at the footing of the last of her notes, the black-on-white words burning into my retina.

"To hear words again. To be able to speak, to communicate as we always did. It has taken nearly a year of work, but we may finally see the end of this nightmare."

I walk over to one of the refrigerator units, staring through the glass at the dull blue illumination within. A blast of icy air hits me as I lift the lid and look at the contents – a frosted metal housing, mostly empty except for a few unused glass vials.

I hold one up to the light, peering at the transparent fluid within. So, this innocuous looking liquid suspension is the cure. From her notes, it's clear that it would be wasted on me – my eardrums had died long before the Shrike, and I'm somewhat reluctant to take her at her word regarding its success with others.

Knowing what I know, it's best disregarded for now. My own research takes precedence. I take one last longing look at it before replacing it in the refrigerator.

I don't think I'd gotten more than an hour into catching up on my own research studies before I'd fallen asleep at the laptop, snoring and drooling in my chair. I had no idea what time it was, other than darkness had begun creeping over as I'd been looking through Alice's notes, and my sleep was fitful and shallow.

I was woken by an agitated Paxton who, the very instant my eyes opened, leaned in and silenced me with a shush gesture. The obvious panic in my expression meant I didn't need to sign my concern.

I don't think we're alone, he signed, stumbling over the words in his urgency.

The room was in darkness, the only light coming from the dull humming luminescence of the open refrigerator. I got to my feet as he trained the rifle around the room, darting the weapon's barrel from shadow to shadow. There was sweat on the boy's brow and he looked more panicked than I'd ever seen him.

I fumbled around for my own pistol before remembering I'd stupidly put it in my backpack which was hanging over the back of the door. I made to walk towards it but Paxton's hand on my shoulder stopped me in my tracks.

His mouth was moving, as though he were muttering away to himself with reassuring phrases.

What did you see? I sign, my eyes nervously darting between Paxton and the door.

He mouths the words as he signs them.

I can hear them in the base.

I sign the next word very carefully, right in front of his wide staring eyes.

Hear?

I know I'd closed the refrigerator. I look over to it, and there's an injection gun lying next to it, an empty vial attached. On my laptop, Alice's notes about her final successes at the base fills the screen.

You used the cure, I sign, panicked.

I need to hear, he replies, so I can protect us both.

He doesn't try to stop me again as I slowly walk towards the door.

What can you hear? I sign, but I already know the answer.

His hands are on his temples, the veins on his head threatening to push out through his skin. His eyes are wild, staring. He doesn't sign the response, but mouths it. It's enough.

They're DRUMMING.

He's pointing the gun at imaginary foes, ones that lurk in the darkened corners of the room. His body jerks erratically at regular intervals, every few seconds, like a violent hiccup.

I know from my studies that his spasms match the beats he can hear. For every drum beat, his body can't help but react in an involuntary mini-seizure for each. My research earlier confirmed my suspicions, that the beats have increased in pace over the last year, and will continue to increase in intensity the closer we get to the source.

The rifle slumps at his side, dangling from its sling, as he tries to sign to me. He's mouthing the words to himself, his fingers moving randomly in front of him as he struggles with his coordination.

I take advantage of that moment, grabbing my rucksack and running out into the corridor. I don't need to know what he was trying to tell me.

I run blindly, not daring to look back. Without the ability to hear, I have no idea whether he's followed me at all, or whether he's fresh at my heels. The exhilaration, the fear, that any moment could be my last. As I ran down dim corridors, I realise I'm in a part of the base I haven't been in yet. I'm beginning to tire and am forced to slow down, but the occasional quick tentative glance behind me shows he's nowhere in sight.

I duck inside an alcove and rest for a few moments, rifling through the contents of my rucksack. It had been open when I'd grabbed it, and I'm sure I felt something fall out of it as I ran from Paxton. Not the pistol, luckily, the weapon's weight keeping it firmly at the bottom of the bag. In fact, everything looks in place.

There's a gentle vibration from my wrist as the Pigeon band dutifully informs me of a sound coming from nearby. The pulse is subtle enough to let me know it's distant, but insistent enough to let me know that it's constant.

The problem is, I have no idea whether the noise is coming from one of the unexplored rooms that surrounds me, or from an approaching Paxton.

"You should take one of the v3 Pigeon Bands, Doctor Kearney," they'd helpfully suggested, "They give additional feedback now, so you know which direction any sounds are coming from."

"Oh no", I insisted, "I've only got used to the Pigeon Band that I've got. Thanks, but no thanks."

Melody, you Luddite idiot.

Still, any room should suffice. The entire complex was spread across a single floor, so I only needed to find a window I could open and then I could make my getaway. Unless, of course, Paxton had lost the remainder of the few marbles he had left and found himself a decent vantage point where he could see all the surrounding grounds whilst armed with his high-powered rifle.

It could end up being one of the shortest getaways of all time.

As I step closer to the closed doorway, the Pigeon band vibrates that little bit stronger. Confident that he can't have got to the room before me, I read that as him approaching from behind and step inside, hurriedly closing it behind me.

I realise my mistake as soon as I step in. From all the rooms I could have chosen, I've wound up in what appears to be a shower block. The only daylight comes from glass bricks set just below the ceiling, too high and too small a gap to escape through. There's a foul smell in here as well, something the room's inadequate ventilation has struggled to shift.

I turn to step out, but the Pigeon band fires a small jolt of electricity across the nerve-endings in my wrist. That implies the noise is coming from inside – or directly outside – the room. The sensation freezes me on the spot and I stand there helplessly waiting for my doom.

Then I feel it. A subtle shifting in the air, the slightest of vibrations rippling across my tensed skin. I step further into the room, cautiously peering around the wall of stained blue tiles that hides whatever is in here.

At first it looks like a pile of rubbish, a heap of old tattered clothes that's been left here to rot. But then it suddenly moves, jerking at the same, as the Pigeon band delivers me a painful zap, ripples passing across the bulks surface. A malformed hand extends, crooked and warped fingers clutching at the tiled floor. Some of the fingers are long and wire-thin, others bloated and stubby. With each pulse on my wrist, a part of it covered by a brown-streaked hood from a coat rises and falls. Whatever it is, it's alive.

Even as I approach it, an ignored part of me is screaming at me to run away. A morbid fascination sees my hand extend towards it, grabbing the fabric of the hood. The rest of my body is arched away and my face contorted into a horrified grimace as I prepare myself.

With a jerk of my wrist, I flick the gathered hood of the material away, an act that uncovers the foul thing writhing beneath the filthy cloth. I step back, almost falling against the tiles, and gasp in horror at the thing on the floor.

The cracked and misshapen dome used to be a head, of that much I'm sure. The sides of it still bear the telltale signs of Shrike infection, cancerous growths clinging like moss around where the ears would have been. The ears and nose have long gone, sealed organically shut and reduced to scarred ridges of muscle and tissue. The mouth is still there though, a gaping and hideous hole enlarged to monstrous proportions, with a purple larvae-like tongue lolling about in the bloodied cavernous recesses. The odd tooth hangs there, yellowing, splintered, and crooked.

With each pulse of the watch, I feel the foetid air burst forth from that foul orifice and polluting the air about me. The slug tongue extends to a point, and then relaxes. The Pigeon band fires a vicious pinprick into my nervous system with each sustained burst of its ghastly din.

It's a small blessing that I can't hear that noise, the sound of it screaming.

The sight of the thing is so horrific – so out of my sphere of normality – that it's almost a relief when Paxton barges into the room. As he unsteadily levels the rifle at me, being threatened the old-fashioned way by a man with a gun almost seems mundane.

He's understandably distracted by what's going on behind me, and he seems unsure what to focus his attention on. The barrel of the gun hastily moves from me to the thing on the ground.

Paxton staggers back, visibly pained, his eyes bloodshot and wide. He's witnessed the full horror that I'm immune to – he's heard the thing scream. He barges past me, slamming me against the wall, and opens fire on the monstrosity spread-eagled across the floor, unleashing the rifles fully-automatic wrath.

I turn away from the strobing muzzle flash but feel every 45mm shot hit its mark, the vibrations rippling through the floor and walls. I feel the trembling of shattering tiles, of fragmented porcelain shards ricocheting against each other.

Splashes of a dark black ichor spatter against me, and I recoil from its touch. Paxton has his back to me, the gun now pointing to the floor. He's breathing heavily, his shoulders raised and lowering exaggeratedly, and the floor is scattered with cracking tiling and black and gold shell casings.

The thing twitches at his feet, the shroud torn away. It's reduced to so much pulped meat now, a mess of fragmented musculature and burst organs. The ruined mouth stretches and puckers and the remaining fingers on its one hand jerk in time to the spasms of Paxton as he stands there, now otherwise motionless.

Then it happens. With each pulse, with each convulsion from Paxton, the dying thing matches the beat. Like macabre stop-motion photography, bones click into life, stretching, knotting. Ruined skin stretches over vanishing wounds, and the thing begins to rise.

I've reached the door by the time it's featureless head is level with Paxton. It resembles a crudely sculpted flesh marionette, asymmetrical and twisted. The skin of the thing is discoloured and bruised, patches of it stretched gossamer thin over still-healing organs. As the knotted trunk of muscle that it uses for an arm reaches out for Paxton's face, blackened barbed points bloodily piercing through the creature's calloused hide, the door has opened and I'm stumbling out.

I feel the boy's scream through the walls. I run, plummeting down corridors and through doors. This time, I don't look back until I'm in the open air and safely away from the base.

I spend twenty minutes tentatively approaching the gates of The Dives, the perpetually guarded man-made barrier of abandoned vehicles and trailers stacked like Jenga blocks, before I realise that it's been abandoned. I simply walk into the Pennines, unhindered.

After spending the best part of an hour scouting through the outskirts of the deserted nearby market town of Richmond, I find a building that will do as 6shelter for the evening. An intact stairwell serves as an adequate mount for a Pigeon sensor, and there's a fire-escape should I be trapped upstairs.

Hidden in the woods, it's remained miraculously un-looted. It was left in a hurry and the occupants sadly weren't the type to keep a full food cupboard, but there's some meager bounty for the taking. A half decent thermos flask replaces the dented water bottle I've been carrying since Blackburn, and there are enough powdered soups and milkshakes to keep me fed for a fortnight.

A handful of still wrapped presents sit beneath a threadbare artificial Christmas tree. For some reason, I leave them undisturbed – as though the occupants could return at any time and life would suddenly return to some semblance of normality like a re-wound clock.

I spend the evening handwriting copious notes by torchlight, finding myself in the oddest of moods. I'm elated that my half-a-year of research has been validated, but equally terrified by what that means.

The popular consensus amongst the scientific community was that the Shrike and deafness and the Drummers were inexorably linked, that one led to the other. During a frustrating evening of theorizing and heavy drinking, I'd formulated a counter-opinion – that it was in fact the deafness that had saved us, that it was the body's mechanism of defending itself.

Whatever the beat was – that unstoppable, perpetual rhythm – it destroyed. To hear it, was to be doomed. To be deaf, was to be safe.

The original inspiration had come from the oddest sources. In the days and weeks immediately following that fateful Christmas day, the God squad had come out in force. American televangelists, blissfully ignorant to how little money would come to matter, milked the situation for all it was worth.

It was Mankind's own fault, scrolled the teleprompter, its purveyor smiling through a mouthful of perfect pearlescent teeth set against a dark tan beneath an expensive wig. For too long, Mankind had ignored the word of God. For only those that are righteous, shall hear His word.

Perhaps the noise was the word of God, she'd joked with Solomon. A voice of condemnation, of chastisement. And to not hear it, was to be spared. Solomon had laughed about it then, only deserting her when he realised the level of her dedication to this theory. They'd fought that night, both their tempers fuelled by some reserves of alcohol they'd found secreted in their bungalow-come-makeshift laboratory.

He'd accused her of not taking him seriously, of laughing at his arguments. I couldn't help it, I'd said, people signing swear words in anger is an inherently comical sight.

He'd gone by the time I'd awoken to a hangover, presumably to head further North to prove me wrong – or to reinforce a more sensible and level-headed science team.

Poor Solomon.

It was the big revelation that he couldn't accept, one that countered every belief he had as a scientist. When you've been deaf all your life, you develop a certain knack for recognising sounds through vibrations – couple that knack with some expensive monitoring equipment to "listen" to the beats ever-present in the air beyond normal frequencies, and you begin to realise something.

I'd insisted that they weren't simple drum beats, some ambient percussive white noise.

It felt like data. It felt like data coming in bursts, the gaps of which were noticeably lessening over time. From a source that, I suspected, lay somewhere in the North of England.

But what kind of data? Certainly nothing that I could interpret – it was far more advanced than any protocol I'd ever encountered.

Was it human-made, an act of bio-terrorism? Little green men, getting their revenge for us corrupting their adolescents by sending them "Johnny B. Goode" through space on the Voyager Golden record?

The word of God, condemning his creation?

Whatever it was doing, to hear it was to be mutated. It was like a string of code, slowly rewriting genetic information. At the periphery, thus far, they'd only seen a minor impact – ear-drums infected, spreading slowly around the head and shoulders, brains blighted.

Here, nearer the epicentre, I'd clearly just witnessed an extreme. It was a theory, but matched my studies. Let's say you have something well along the road to infection, used to this slow drip-feed of ultrasonic data, suddenly "cured" by Alice and her team. The lucky patient gets to receive the previously filtered data in all its unfettered, raw glory. And what you end up with is the blasphemy from the shower block.

Would this be what happened to us all, in time?

In my dreams, I'm visited by Paxton's ghost. He's a twisted corpse, limbs held together by the flimsiest of gristle and sinew. As we open the presents beneath the tree, eagerly ripping red and golden paper away from board games, jumpers, and toiletries, he feels compelled to confess something to me. I wasn't entirely honest about being separated from my squadron, he signs – even in dreams, I remain resolutely deaf – but I ran away when they were attacked by Drummers.

I'm fully aware I'm dreaming, and my subconscious had obviously pieced that together from our brief interactions. I'm about to tell him that it's okay when he runs to the window, staring out through it.

Can you hear that? He signs, his words carefully chosen.

I can, I reply. Because I can.

My eyes are barely even open by the time I'm awake and dragging pieces of equipment from my bag to confirm what I'm experiencing. I can feel it in the air; a paradigm shift, as though something incredible has happened - another chapter begun.

Three separate checks confirm my fears. It's either an incredible coincidence, or fate has chosen some particularly apt timing. It's Christmas morning, exactly one year since the beat started, and the graphs confirm that it's now a solid single noise, a stream of digital Morse code. The military tattoo has become a drum-roll.

So, to honour him, pa rum pum pun pum. When we come.

Merry Christmas.

Cross Fell, they call it. The highest mountain in the Pennine Hills, all eight hundred and ninety metres of it. It had eluded me for so long, but now it takes just some cursory triangulation to get the source, almost as though it doesn't feel the need to hide from me anymore.

Is it broadcasting to the world? Or are there more sites like this, dotted around the globe? And are they all, like this one, screaming?

The landscape leading up the ridge is a graveyard of abandoned vehicles. Smart cars, sports cars, family saloons, and larger vehicles like buses and coaches are the first casualties, stuck in ditches, sprawled across rocks, or stranded on terrain too steep to climb. As I draw closer, I pass hardier transport – Jeeps, Land Rovers, 4 x 4's – they've all met their match on this barren wilderness. Lastly, at points where even I struggle to navigate, the final resting place of the last of the metal behemoths; armoured cars, military Jeeps, and even a tank.

I see and keep my distance from the occasional Drummer, but they seem unconcerned by my presence, or the company of other infected around them. They're staring at that distant peak, relentlessly placing one foot in front of the other, one foot in front of the other, one foot in front of the other.

For the most part, they seem physically unaffected by the drums. From the dozen or so I see, only one is abnormally shaped, dragging a huge arm the length and thickness of an elephant's trunk behind it on its trek up to the summit. Their muscles jerk rhythmically in unison, spasming like poorly animated videogame characters.

A dense hill fog is settling over the dull earth, soaking me to the skin. I'm ill-prepared for this trek but something compels me to keep walking. Not the same thing that compels the Drummers, but we are equally as driven.

As the afternoon turns into early evening, visibility becomes poorer. The mist thickens, whorls of languid grey vapour hugging the earth. Whilst distracted, I almost collide with a Drummer – with panicked breaths and cursing my stupidity, I rest and let it vanish into the murky haze ahead.

I can feel vibrations beneath my feet, tiny seismic shifts from an ever-present humming, like the operations of some vast, foul, stygian machinery. I place both my palms on the damp earth and feel it undulate. I try to concentrate on it, and not on the clicking spidery thing that clatters past me into the void.

In ancient times, this region was known as Fiend's Fell and was believed to be the haunt of evil spirits. It now feels that Saint Augustine's blessings have long since faded.

It's only as the dense smog clears that I realise I'm just part of a crowd. Now dozens of Drummers walk alongside me up the steep grass and stone embankment, all focused on the path ahead. Some falter and stumble, dashing themselves on the sharpened gravel, but their kin simply step on or over them in ignorance to their plight.

    I pass two who must have toppled from much higher, a male and female lying intertwined, limbs at obscene angles and egg-shell skulls part-caved in. They twitch in desperation, strangers locked together until they rot.

    Jack fell down and broke his crown, and Jill came tumbling after.

    The mutations are stronger now, more pronounced. Perhaps they're metamorphosing en route, deforming and shifting with each leg of the journey. Some are crawling on all fours like apes, some dragging themselves along with hook like appendages, some scurrying on fresh barbed limbs.

    There's a certain beauty to it, a uniqueness to every one of them. Simple symmetrical human shapes contorted to bizarre flesh sculptures, none the same. Like evolution, some have failed and are left abandoned. Others flourish, hurrying to the snow streaked peak.

    There is no fear as I walk amongst them. They have a greater goal now than confronting me, and I'm disregarded in their new priorities. I look around myself, down the peak, at the crowds that follow in my wake. Hordes of them, gathering in numbers, all with one singular purpose.

And then, in front of me, a wall of them. The crowd is mostly halted, bottlenecked by something ahead. Too late I realise that the momentum of those behind me will sweep me into the amassed crowds, and I look about in a panic.

Their numbers are too great, and I struggle to find a gap to make my way to safety. The crowds behind push against me, and I'm forced into the misshapen throng. My shoulder barges into one of the Drummers, and it briefly turns to face me.

It's a ghastly, tilted thing of skinless musculature, with only one small, single remaining patch of flesh set atop its red and glistening head – a lone green eye that stares through me glinting and blinking. I grimace and retreat, shuddering in grim recognition.

No, it can't be Paxton.

The crowd heaves, rippling like a disturbed pond, and I'm carried forward. Spider legs with tiny furred paws brush against my shoulders, and I recoil away. I'm pushed into a wall of flesh- mounted eyes atop stunted limbs barely capable of carrying their weight, and they glare at me, accusingly.

I hear my own laughter echoing inside my skull, the last vestiges of panicked sanity pouring from me like sweat. I can see a hole in the cliffside, a twisted rock scar, and realise the hordes ahead of me are in single file, slowly marching in.

I'm reminded of the legends of the children of Hamelin, pulled into the underworld by the rhythmic beats of the Pied Piper.

It's like a precise military march; feet, claws, and pincers moving in perfect synchronization. One step, two step, one step, two step, one step, two step.

Staggering out into the open, my stumbling legs break the beat.

They all stop. One by one, as though instructed to do so by the conductor of an orchestra, they turn to face me. A Mexican wave of misshapen faces. An array of eyes, antennae and proboscises turn their focus away from the cliff and to me.

There's nowhere to run, and they're upon me. There is no urgency – there's nowhere for me to run to, and they seem aware of that. They advance, and reach out for me. I'm carried above their heads on a carpet of limbs of all textures, sizes, and shapes, and being carried towards the jagged wound in the cliff.

I'm lowered down, exalted now at the lead of the queue. The crowds gather behind me, paused. They don't push against me – it feels like I have all the time in the world, but the wall of mangled and reworked flesh makes it obvious that I won't be leaving the way I came in.

The rhythm is more obvious here, thudding a snare drum heartbeat against the cave walls. I can feel the pulses travelling up through my feet and across my exhausted form. I'm struggling to formulate complete thoughts as even my teeth chatter from the dull yet insistent tempo.

It's coming from beneath me, that much is apparent now. It's like there's a drummer at the heart of the world, providing a percussive accompaniment to the end of times. A clarion call from the Earth itself.

Ahead a luminescent pool laps lazily against the rock. It fills the cave with a rare humidity, and sections of it bubble and steam as though it's oozing from the planet's core. It's thick and gelatinous, and feels ancient, primordial even. Like the chemical-laden soup from where we all sprung, here again at the end.

One of the Drummers is in front of me, staring down at the lapping waters that gather around his cloven ankles. His skin is coated with a vibrant sheen of reflective scales, the light emanating from below him glinting off the surface, refracting as he steps deeper in.

He seems to stumble, falling to one side. At first, I think he's lost his balance but then it becomes clear as I see the effect on the rest of him. He's being absorbed into it, dissolving painlessly into the primal broth. Flesh slides from his form, congealing about him. He remains calm, unmoved. The thick islands of detritus that drift lazily across the surface of the gelatinous pool are biological matter.

It's then, at the end, that my resolve leaves me, and I turn to run. The Drummers move as one, flooding into the cave as an impenetrable wall.

There is little pain. The same cruelly curved barbs that take my eyes act with surgical precision, cauterizing damaged flesh. The ravages that surge across the geography of my twitching form are quick and total.

I continue, blind and deaf, the remainder of my senses numbed.

The last sensation of my mortality is the warmth of the fluid against my dying nerves, the last vestige of my dying senses telling me that they're lowering me into the waters. The pool claims not only my form, but also my soul. That mankind should briefly burst out into a myriad of complex, beautiful and horrific forms at the very end before settling into this fate, this parliament of total harmony.

I hear their voices, and I feel their heartbeats. One rhythm shared by all, and then the most extraordinary sense of relief. They - we - have but one shared thought.

If I had words, I would tell of it.

11. Pipers Piping
Matthew Cash

When I first saw the ad in the Daily Record I thought, "Fuck me, they desperate for an audience or what?"

The Edinburgh Royal Military Tattoo, the traditional annual extravaganza that sucked tourists from all corners of the world like a weathered old pisshead draining the glass for the last few dregs of cheap shitey lager.

Be proud of your country, that's what the advert said, like we weren't already. I fucking love Scotland me. I guess they wanted more of us natives going to one of the country's largest events rather than millions of people from around the world.

I usually just watch the show on the BBC whilst having a carry out and a bevvy. But this year I found myself filling out the wee competition form in the newspaper and sending it off. It was freepost and all.

Well, the days wound on and on, posters began to be slapped up everywhere advertising the Fringe festival which usually coincided with the Tattoo. Showmen from some of the more zany acts would cruise the Royal Mile in their fancy garb telling all and sundry to flock to their shows.

It was a good time of the year, I didn't mind the tourists, it brought some culture to the place, and last year I pulled a couple of yank lassies that came in my local so it wasn't too bad for me.

Anyways, I put it down to drink, drugs, too much cheese before bedtime, the usual suspects, but for a few weeks after filling out that wee form I started having weird dreams.

Now, I hadn't really been to the castle since I was a nipper. My dad took us just before he took himself off to England with some scuzzy yo-yo knickered floozy. But, being a resident of this fine city meant it was always up there looking down at us. The castle is bloody impressive, sitting up there scowling down at the city, acting the hard man up on its mountainous pedestal.

So even though I hadn't been up there since I was a laddie I was up there again in the first of these recurring dreams.

12days Of Christmas:2017

It was night time and I was standing at the walls next to one of them big cannon jobbies, the ones they use to fire at one o'clock each day. I was taking in the view of the city at night, the lights, the monument protruding like a space rocket out of a Giger painting, and it was fucking beautiful. That was when I heard bagpipes, not so strange I hear you say, being in Scotland's finest city and all, but it took me by surprise. It sounded funny, distorted like. I turned and wandered the grounds to find the source. It didn't take me long; I mean bagpipes aren't exactly your most inconspicuous musical instrument. The castle was deserted, something I thought odd. Places like these should be secured twenty-four seven, but nonetheless I walked towards the source of the cacophony. As I got closer I could see the piper standing on one of the walls, his back to me, the pipes tucked under his left arm. I was impressed but not too surprised Scotland the brave and all that, to see him standing up there without any safety harnesses or anything above what is probably a several hundred feet drop. I may have over or underestimated that measurement but I don't really care, I'm no mathematician. It was a long way down, enough to make you go from man to jam in under a minute.

I noticed there was something weird about him, fanning out behind the back of his head was a spray of something, a semi-transparent headdress, like when you see fashion models with stuff sticking out of their hair, feathers and shit.

Whether it was the moon poking out from behind a cloud or just some convenient dream coincidence, a dim glow illuminated his fucked up tiara. It was the whacking great glistening hole in the back of his head that gave it away. A headshot bullet wound in suspended animation. The spray at the back, shards of skull, matted clumps of hair, chunks of brain, blood splatter frozen like red jewels, crimson pearls, molten wax seals with a bullet's stamp. All the time he played the damn pipes oblivious to this, surely fatal, head wound. I recognised the tune. Scotland the Brave.

Obviously I'm a rational man, it was a trick, a marketing ploy for one of the festival acts, a costume. I leant against the wall and checked out his front. They had done a really good job, made him look like he'd been in a car crash or something. He was blackened and red. His fancy clothes melded to his skin, the front of his kilt had been burnt away and there was just a mess of gore from his chest downwards, he wore his entrails like a shrivelled tatty leather apron.

"Awesome costume brother," I shouted up at him. He ignored me, not even a wink, but then again he didn't look like he had any eyes. One was just a blood filled hole and the other a crisp black cavern.

12days Of Christmas:2017

It's weird, even though I could see no one other than the lone piper all around me, the deafening cries of thousands of people woke me from my dream.

Turns out it was my clock radio alarm playing some upbeat hip hop bullshit to get me the hell out of bed. I always made sure I tuned it into the most annoying radio station so as to piss me off enough to get me out of bed.

I punched the bastard, it was novelty pish, designed like a punchbag, and shuffled through to the kitchen. That was when I saw the letter on the mat.

I picked it up frowning like I'd never seen a bloody envelope before, and slit it open with my thumb. A posh embossed ticket to the Edinburgh Military Tattoo.

"Fuck me," I thought. I'd never won a thing in my whole life, even in sports at school the only thing I managed to catch was athletes' foot in the changing rooms. I was stoked man, really stoked. There was nothing else in the envelope aside from a brief compliments card. It made me happy but I think I've already said that, so even though the date was still a few weeks away I went out after breakfast and bought myself a new shirt.

The big day came and I splashed out a bit on a few drams of quality whisky from one of the posher places on the Mile, I thought why not man, it wasn't everyday people like me got to go anywhere nice.

    I found a nice restaurant, had a blinding steak and chips, you could tell it was posh nosh, Gordon Blue or whatever the fuck it's called, because the dinner came on a chopping board and the chips had the skins on still. It was lush, especially with the whisky afterwards.

    When I left the place I walked up the Mile and up Castle Hill towards, well, the castle. Hundreds of people were already flocking in that direction, groups from every corner of the globe, a hive of activity with the buzz of dozens of different languages. Made a change from the only person being unintelligible I came into contact with being Fred the jakey from outside the bookies, I can tell you. It was nice, different.

    The seating in the Esplanade had undergone a big change a few years back but I couldn't tell the difference, looked the same as it did on the fucking telly only way bigger.

    I was shown to my seat by some young spirited usher and just sat there taking in the experience.

    Where I was sat was dead centre like, opposite the castle. Best seats in the house brother, not far from the front either.

12days Of Christmas:2017

    I sat whilst the place filled up, probably maximum capacity, every seat seemed full. A bunch of female backpacker types were sat next to me, I'd didn't know where they were from, they weren't that talkative to me, even when I said "hello", but whatever, I wasn't going to let in shit in my shower if you know what I mean.

    Finally the show started with hundreds of dancers from, I forget where they said now, Zimbabwe or somewhere, and they did this cool tribal piece with yelling and drums.

    After that there were some wee lassie dancers from Skye and the islands up north, really beautiful man.

    The New Zealand fellas, the Maori is it? The natives came on with all their gear and did one of them mad dances they do at the rugby. A haka. Scary bastards but purely belter too, I was close enough to see the wee veins in their heads pop up when they yelled.

    Things started getting more traditional when the Scots Guard paraded with their brasses and pipes and tartan, that was more like it. They played a medley of all the greats. I hoped to Christ no one would try and be modern like that year they went and did that Gangnam Style dance, that had been fucking ridiculous.

    At what I guessed was halfway through their set, two almighty fucking crashes that sounded like the Devil farting came from each side of the arena and everything went white for a second.

I instinctively ducked into the footwell, as chaos surrounded me. My first thoughts were the obvious ones. And it turns out I wasn't wrong. Terrorists.

Panic everywhere, people were screaming and clambering over the seating to flee the castle grounds. I risked a peep over the seat in front of me and wish to God I hadn't.

The seating up each side of the arena had bloody great holes blown in them like an asteroid had shot through the place. Debris from the blasts was everywhere, crowds on the sides of the blast zones writhed like maggots to get away from the fires that were dotted about. There were pieces of people everywhere, all over the Esplanade. A lot of the performers had taken the worst of the blast but those lucky to survive it were busy trying to help their fallen comrades. It was a battle zone.

Then I saw the lone piper, way up at the undamaged part near the main castle. A voice boomed over the speakers, those that hadn't been destroyed. "Keep calm and head towards the piper."

The fellow was limping badly, one of his legs was red and ruined, and no one was paying attention to him even though he waved his arms and shouted. So he took up the bagpipes and began to play them. This poor heroic fucker played wonderfully, it was in his blood this beautiful, beautiful bastard. He had been on fire for fuck sake and there he was playing, trying to round up people from every nation like some beautiful bloody ginger Scottish Jesus.

People had cottoned on and slowly but surely the frantic multitudes began moving in his direction.

That was when another threat presented itself.

From out of the crowds came the sound of rapid gunfire and more screaming.

People started rushing around and running back towards me. I spotted the gunman just before I threw myself back to the floor out of the way of trampling feet. Aside from generic t-shirt and jeans that was all I noticed about him.

More gunfire came from further down where the crowds were rushing from the piper back towards the main entrance.

I'm not a religious man, but if this was for a holy cause then I would hate to meet the God that condoned this shit.

One of the young students who had been sat near me stood on the steps, looking for her friends. I yanked at her trouser leg for her to get down when a bullet whipped through the air, ruffled her hair and blew her brains out of her forehead. My scream was but a wank in the ocean compared to the hell-noise around me.

I hid, I cried, I feared for my stupid useless fucking life, as thousands of people were being mowed down by crazy bastards.

A break in gunfire.

That was when I heard the piper still playing; he was joined by others, a signal for people to still come their way, that together they would be stronger.

The gunfire recommenced and I thought of my miserable existence and the people being killed all around me. I belonged with them. I was nothing.

One of the gunmen was now stood right beside me, a black machine gun in his hands, bullets showering the running people ahead of him, smiling as he shouted something in another language.

I got the bottle of whisky stowed in my pocket, twisted the cap off and took a large swig. Might as well die with a belly full of whisky. Maybe the fumes on the breath of my dead body would mask the reek of piss in my pants.

Then something took over me and I found myself leaping up and smashing the cunt over the head with the half-filled bottle. He hadn't known what had hit him and the fear that he may get up again once he had fallen made me go a little bit crazy. I stomped on that fucker's head until there was nothing left.

I shook, I had not expected that, but a fighting part of me had been ignited, if I was going to be killed by one of these bastards I was sure going to try taking at least another one down first. I grabbed his gun and a spare magazine I saw protruding from his trouser pocket. I didn't know what the hell I was doing.

I crouched back down and peeked over the seats towards the gunfire. I made out at least three other gunmen at different positions, open firing on innocent people.

My heart was still rampant from beating the fella to death; I wasn't worried whether or not I'd be arrested. I doubted that I'd last the following ten minutes.

I crawled along the footwell behind the row of seats over handbags dropped in the melee. Every now and then I popped my head up to see what was happening down on the Esplanade. The crowds were rushing to a band of determined pipers and the surviving military men began to skirt around them fencing them in. They were trying to protect the people but all the marching ones had were empty decorative rifles with fixed bayonets. The gunmen cut a swathe through the people running towards what they thought was safety. I saw mothers, fathers, sisters, brothers, sons and daughters from all around the world being gunned down by these deluded heartless bastards.

 A few other people, Japanese I think, had taken to hiding behind the seats like me and shrieked when they saw me crawling towards them with a bloody great gun. I motioned for them to stay put but they were just frightened. The father grabbed his wife and the two wee bairns and legged it down the steps away from me.

 The gunman pacing this part of the arena swivelled his weapon towards them and I saw the two bairns' faces explode all over their parents before the spray of bullets obliterated their legs and they tumbled down onto the bodies of their dead children.

 I ran at the bastard.

 I've never fired a gun before, I mean I've played your video games and stuff but that's the most I've done. I wasn't expecting the kick it gave when I pointed it at the fucker and pulled the trigger. The thing buzzed in my hands and a series of red spots like blooming flowers dotted the man's white shirt and went up in the air as the force of the thing made me shake. I took my finger from the trigger and my arms felt numb.

I saw the other two signal towards me and one of them moved across the rows in my direction.

I continued towards the Esplanade with the intention of handing over the weapon to one of the soldiers, the brave bastards who were trying to keep the people safe. The bombs had blown great holes in the stands, debris was dropping off the sides, I think some were actually people jumping. I could hear sirens over the screaming and the whir of approaching helicopters. I hoped to hell they would hurry up.

The gunman fired at me and I dropped to the floor, the bullets missing me by inches as they zipped past my ears and made mincemeat of the padding in the seats. I stuck the gun over the back of a chair, aimed it in his general direction and fired it once more. I risked a look, hoping I had struck lucky. I hadn't, the fucker, and now he had seen I was armed, decided to spend the last of his time picking off the defenceless.

The gunmen worked their way towards the crowd of people in the centre of the Esplanade where the pipers still played, and the wounded were dragged amongst the debris from the bombs. The soldiers stood firm and defiant, but there wasn't that many of them to protect that number of people. I remember thinking that if only they would all rush the gunmen as a collective, they could take them down.

The gunmen laughed and shouted more gibberish as they stormed across the Esplanade, reloading from spare clips hidden about their clothing. A few of the brave soldiers did do as I had thought, a group of about four rushed towards the gunman nearest to them but the bastard cut them down in a heartbeat.

I had lost all self-concern then, I just ran down the steps towards the murderous cunts.

I was probably few hundred yards from them; people had started abandoning the crowd, trampling over one another, doing horrific things just to try and save their own backs but to no avail.

Then one of the bastards turned on me.

I dropped to the floor but not before I felt something whack against my arm just above the elbow. I had been shot. It fucking hurt. I rolled across the littered ground, dead and injured people everywhere.

One of the soldiers had taken the opportunity to attack the gunman whilst his attention was on me. I cheered as I saw the guy thrust his bayonet straight through the bastard's back and saw the tip burst from his chest. The soldier pushed the gunman to the ground and was instantly decapitated by the remaining one's fire.

I picked up the gun and ran towards the last gunman.

He was being more careful with his shots, taking out all the soldiers until none were left.

I could hear and see the armies of police approaching the entrance but wondered how many more people would be slain before the gunman was either taken down or turned the gun on himself. The fucker started on the row of pipers who stood steadfast until the bullets tore them apart, the defiant warriors refusing to buckle and surrender to their enemy. Scotland the brave, man. The gunman stopped to reload. I sped up, seizing the moment. All that was remained were those who wondered how many more bullets the man had left and whether it would be them or a loved one who would be taken. Standing above the frightened crowd, the lone piper. The one from my fucking dreams. As I got closer I saw the poor fella was in a right state, badly burnt and barely standing but something in the poor bastard made him want to play his pipes until they inflated with his last breath and sung the notes of his dying.

"Scotland the brave!" I screamed in a war cry as I ran towards the last gunman. This is it, I thought as he turned his weapon on me but his gun got stuck. I ploughed into him and as we went down his gun went off and the piper stopped, the bagpipes giving one last pathetic wheeze. "No!" I cried and looked down at the laughing muttering bastard. He didn't care, he expected to die, was all part of the cunt's bigger plan, whether it be a deluded promise to some Creator, or just some brainwashed cult. There was no fear in the fucker's eyes at all. I was going to kill the bastard so fucking much.

I raised the hard butt of the gun above his head, his face covered in blood spatter and perspiration, smiling, nodding.

I used the weapon to pound the living shit out of the fucker's arms until they were nothing but rags on the dirt. I dragged the cunt by the ankles across the Esplanade, screaming, "Scotland the brave!" I think I had gone a wee bit nuts by then. People looked at me like I was a hero or something, I didn't feel like one. I passed the lone piper; bullet wound in his left eye just like in my dream, and dragged the fucker towards the approaching police and medical crews. As we met I could hear the chanting of the people behind me spur me on even though the blood coming out of my arm was making me giddy.

Scotland the brave.

Scotland the brave.

Scotland the brave.

10. Lords Leaping
Mark Nye

Cold air swept over Martin's face. The world as he knew it had been inexorably changed on the day he became a Lord. Nothing had prepared him for the life he now lived. The horrors he bore witness to. He lifted his head and sought the skyline. Tear filled eyes watched amber towers rocket into the sky. It could have been so glorious, he thought. If only I'd run. If only she hadn't found us, found me.

Three hours ago...

Gemma gave Martin a sympathetic look. Normally it would have worked to placate his foul mood, but not today. He could see the unforgiving air of smugness behind it, her I'm better than you and I've won attitude shining through. He shot her back a nasty look, fully aware that it was wasted. She stood, hands on hips, almost daring the rest of the room to disagree with her. Her right foot tapped on the tiled floor. 'Well Martin?'

Silence was his answer. The silent vote had sealed his fate and he knew there was no arguing with it. His shoulders slumped and he relaxed his stance. He considered making one final plea, a sympathetic appeal to the rest of the group. But it was useless. He was the last of the Ten Lords. The others hoped if they expelled him from the group that the creatures would stop attacking. They had already sacrificed seven other Lords. They made them jump from the roof of the ten storey building. But the creatures kept coming. Martin was the tenth, and last, Lord. The only reason he hadn't been sacrificed with the rest was that the other survivors needed him to scavenge for food. But he had come back empty-handed after his last sortie into the streets. The howls and laughter of the creatures had grown louder over the next day.

In the morning, as Martin slept, Gemma called a silent vote, a vote to expel or sacrifice him to the creatures. Some of the young and the elderly had grown to like Martin and the vote ended in a tie. A small girl named Rachel held the last vote in her hand. She handed it to Gemma and she read out the verdict.

'Expulsion.'

Gemma woke Martin and informed him he had to leave the haven. Everyone in the room stared at the floor as he looked at them. The only person to meet his gaze was Rachel. She shuffled over to him and hugged his leg.

Placing a hand on the top of her head, Martin's eyes met Gemma's. He realised it was the only way to save the rest of the group and he nodded at her. But through the sympathetic gaze he could see the smugness in her eyes.

Martin pushed Rachel away from his leg and headed for the barricaded door. He worked his way through the silent group, reaching the table and pushing it out of the way. He drew back the deadbolts and a withered hand landed on his shoulder. An old man called Geoffrey gave him a weak smile and pushed a battered rucksack into his hands. 'For your journey, my friend.'

Martin returned the smile and placed a hand on Geoffrey's arm. 'Thank you.'

With a final glance at the group Martin opened the door and slid through. He heard the bolts slamming across as the door shut behind him, followed by the table being put back into place. He couldn't believe it. Gemma had ensured he had no place to return to, no sanctuary from the dead.

He reached into the rucksack and scrambled around through the meagre provisions. It contained two old t-shirts, some stale bread and two apples. Underneath the clothes he found a small flashlight. He smiled. Thank you Geoffrey. Flipping the switch on the side, the small torch illuminated the hallway. Dark corridors ran in either direction. He shone the tiny light on the sign in front of him. It showed the emergency stairs were to the left.

Martin secured the rucksack across his back and headed down the hall. He had no destination in mind; he just wanted to get out of the building. Nearing the end, he swept the light over the walls again. The passage was devoid of any light, the power stations had died not long after The Event. Another sign indicated the stairs were again to the left. Turning down the hallway he scanned the light over the walls and saw a little green box. Its pale light shone over the doorway. The eerie glow grew brighter as he neared the doorway to the stairs.

He placed his hand on the rail and pushed. The door popped open with ease and slid back into the dark. Stepping through, Martin passed the small light over the stairs. He flashed it up and down the stairway. The flashlight flickered in his hand. He watched it helplessly as it went out. Shit. He smacked it on the palm of his hand a few times, shook it, begged it, but to no avail. He was in the dark, alone.

He could feel something.

Martin shook his head. No. It was just his imagination. Nothing was in the dark with him. But still he had felt something, sensed something. He gasped. Something warm brushed against his ankle. The flashlight slipped from his hand and fell to the stairs. It bounced on the concrete, making a sound that seemed far too loud within the confines of the stairway. He held his breath. The small torch reached the next landing and rattled to a stop against the wall. Silence fell. Nothing happened.

Martin placed his foot upon the descending stair. An echo of laughter drifted up from down below. He froze and bit his lip to stop himself from crying out. Without the light he was blind, straining to see the faintest outline of anything in the stairway. He leaned over the edge of the railing. Moonlight flooded the lower levels. Shit, the door. Shadows flickered across the open hallway. Backing away from the edge, Martin turned and headed up the stairs. He took them two at a time, his footfalls silent in the dark.

He stretched his hands outwards, one running along the bannister and the other with fingertips brushing the wall. His feet thumped the stairs, his heart pounding in his ears. A few minutes passed without incident and he relaxed, slowing his pace and conserving his energy. He slowed to a walk and waited for the drumbeat in his head to subside. I am the last of the Ten, should I should lie down and die? He stopped walking and leant against the railing. Peering into the darkness, he could not see the light from the doorway anymore and the laughter had stopped.

No, I won't give her the satisfaction. Gemma's smug face floated across his mind. He pushed away from the wall and headed up the stairs with a newfound determination. It was all he needed, something to aim for. Lord Armfield had once told him…

Armfield was dead.

It had begun with Lord Armfield. The first of the Ten to die. The walls of his office were splattered with crimson when his receptionist had found him. His severed head placed upon the top of the flagpole in the corner of his room. His body forty stories below, spread over the pavement in a kaleidoscope of blood and bone. After his death, the end began. The dead rose from their graves and converged on the living. Families ate family, friends ate foe. The whole world became a buffet for the buried.

Lord Nichols died next. The police had arrived at the local swimming baths after a silent alarm was tripped. They found Lord Nichols' head on the top diving board, fifty metres high. His body was floating in the red water below. The force of impact with the water had split his torso from throat to testicle. They took days to remove each piece of him from the filtration unit. His death acted as catalyst for the dead to evolve. They learned to use tools.

Martin figured it wouldn't be long before someone let slip about the Ten Lords and their purpose, and he was right. The remaining eight Lords had holed up in the apartment block with the rest of the survivors. One night Lord Jefferson and Lord Chase were whispering, trying to figure out how to stop the impending apocalypse. One of the other residents had overheard and got up to confront them. In minutes, the entire group was awake and the identity of the Lords was out in the open. All except one was ousted in the argument. Martin. There was panic. Gemma convinced the group that a sacrifice would appease any god listening and stop the creatures. The group turned on the remaining seven and forced them up to the roof and made them jump.

The creatures kept coming. Each day they got smarter and faster. They communicated with one another. It didn't take Gemma long to figure that there was one Lord left and who it was. If it hadn't been for the fact he had become useful, she would have killed him there and then. But once he outlived his usefulness, she turned on him and revealed him to the group.

Martin fumbled along the wall, all the courage and vitriol he had built up dissipated into the dark. For the first time in his life, he understood what being alone meant. Unhooking the rucksack from his shoulders, he brought it round to his front and rifled through it, hoping to find something he missed the first time. He brushed the clothes to the side and felt something hard tap against the back of his hand. He fumbled around the outside of the bag and found an external pocket. He pulled the zip back and thrust his hand in, his fingers closed around a small oblong, metal object. Pulling it out, his fingertips found a small button, and he pushed it. With silent ease the object vibrated once in his hand and he felt a spring uncoil. He ran his finger up the item, his nails sliding over the knife edge. The blade bit into the skin and he yelped in the dark.

A knife, perfect. He sucked the end of his finger. If he got swarmed it would be useless, but it offered a small comfort.

Martin's hand on the wall suddenly hit nothing but air. He was at the top of the stairs, almost on the roof. He opened the door and squinted against the sudden brightness of the moon, trying to judge his surroundings. He saw a few chairs against the edge of the wall, where the residents would come on a warm day to enjoy the sun. It had been a while since he spent any prolonged amount of time outside and he relished the feel of a fresh breeze across his skin.

Martin paused, mentally preparing himself for whatever lay ahead. He had to get across to the next building; he couldn't bring himself to go back down the stairs and beg Gemma to let him back in.

He headed towards the nearest edge, the edge where the group had thrown the other Lords off. He leaned over the lip of the roof and looked out across the city. Fires burned on every street, sending black towers of smoke and soot spiralling into the sky. His eyes followed the edge of the wall and rested on a metal fire escape going down the far side. With a smile creasing his face, Martin headed for it. Something laughed behind him.

A low, weak moan came from the same direction. Martin turned, torn between sprinting for the fire escape and protecting the children hidden five floors below. The moaning came again, weaker than before but followed by a crazed chuckle. He wanted to run, but some noble compulsion forced him to stand his ground.

There was no more moaning, only the rasping giggle floating across the rooftop. It reminded him of Rachel when he told her silly jokes to calm her asthma attacks.

Thud.

Something landed close by.

Thud.

A wooden board landed at his feet.

THUD.

The door to the roof exploded in a shower of wooden splinters. Martin sank to his knees as the largest creature he had ever seen squeezed its way onto the roof. Muscles rippled across every arm and leg. Two little eyes sat sunk inside its square jawed head. Moonlight glimmered across its bald skull. Martin's gaze scanned the creature's torso. An amalgamation of human faces stared back at him, each skin mask stitched to the next by a thick black thread. Dull eyes stared through him, unseeing.

The creature raised its wrinkled snout to the sky and took a deep sniff of the air. 'Ah, here you be,' it said. Its booming voice bounced around the rooftop. 'Someone wants word with you.'

Stepping to the side of the doorway, the undead monstrosity squatted on its haunches and waited. From the dark of the destroyed door, a girl appeared. She floated through the air, shimmering, almost glowing, naked in the moonlight. But she wasn't glowing. It was her skin. She was astonishingly white, near translucent. Martin thought he could see a blue network of veins beneath.

Impossible.

The girl floated towards him until she was right in front of his face. Martin's heart beat wild in his chest. This was her. Dark lips blossomed on her face in a miasma of cracked skin, contrasting with the whiteness of her flesh. Large chunks of translucent meat sloughed off of her body to land silent on the roof. Each chunk regenerated in an instant with a paler patch of skin. Her eyes met Martin's and her smile grew wider, lips stretching impossibly wide on such a small face.

Martin flinched under her piercing gaze and turned away. The bleach white corpse tilted her head to the side, assessing him. He shrunk even further under her studious glare.

'You are the last, Lord Martin,' she hissed in a matter-of-fact tone.

Martin nodded.

The girl let out a giggle and twirled her white hair between her fingers, her brow furrowed.

'Now, what am I going to do with you?'

'I-I don't know.' Martin hung his head. The girl bared her jagged grey and yellow teeth, tinged with the blood of her last meal.

'You know me Martin. It was you and the other nine that created me.'

The girl reached out with both hands and cradled his head between them. The full implication of the Ten Lords actions struck Martin across the face. She applied a little pressure, just enough pain to bring him back to the present.

'Come on Martin. You remember. You and the so-called Ten Lords did this. You sacrificed me so you could have unlimited wealth and power. But do you realise what happens when you make a deal with the devil? Do you know what happens when you sacrifice your own sister?' A slight hysterical tone edged into the rasp of her voice, a pleading whine for the answers she desired.

'Sandra?' Martin looked incredulously at his sister's face. Everything was there. The button nose that always wrinkled when she laughed, the small scar above her left eye from where she had fallen face first on the trampoline when she was five. The ears that were too large for her small head. 'Sandy?'

'Don't you dare call me that,' Sandra roared, pushing her brother's head away with such force he fell on his back. 'You and the other Lords murdered me. You killed me for your own gains.'

'No. It wasn't me, it was...'

'Lies,' Sandra screamed. 'You were part of the Ten. You were there that night. You plunged a dagger into me; it was in YOUR hand.'

'I-I'm sorry Sandy.'

'No. Do you understand why I saved you until last? I was giving you the chance to figure it out, to find out why the dead had risen. Why the Ten Lords started the apocalypse.'

'I don't know. I didn't get what the fuck was happening.' Martin pushed himself up from the floor.

'Well, allow me to educate you on the fine print. Your deal had a small negation clause, just a tiny thing. If any of the Ten murdered each other to gain more money or power then the deal became void. I was released from the pit and allowed to seek my retribution any way I please. Are you still with me?'

Martin nodded, dumbfounded.

'Because here is where it gets good,' Sandra smiled. 'Lord Carter killed Donald Armfield. Bet you didn't realise that. He bought shares in Armfield Incorporated and became the majority shareholder. By killing Donald he gained control of his company and planned to sell it off in pieces to make more money. Thus the deal became void, and I was set free. Did you wonder where the dead came from? No? Do you remember all those zombie movies you let me watch when we were children? Well, hello brother.' Sandra curtsied.

'Stop,' rasped Martin.

'Stop? Did you stop when I pleaded with you not to plunge that knife into me?' Sandra shouted.

Nothing happened for a moment. Then Sandra's cold purple lips pressed against Martins. His breath vanished. He kicked out, his foot passing right through his sister. Her left hand grabbed his hair and forced his face onto hers. Martin's left hand darted to his pocket, drawing out the knife. He jabbed blindly at the floating corpse. The blade slid into his sister's flesh, eliciting a small gasp. The smell of rot and decay filled the roof. He yanked down on the blade, trying to pull it free. It broke.

Martin stopped struggling. There was something in his sister's touch he had longed for, yearned for. Unbidden images of Sandra riding his stiff cock flashed through his mind. Her lips wrapped around his hard member. The broken corpses of the other Lords shifting beneath them as they fucked. And then he was falling.

Sandra looked down at him on his knees, once more wearing the impossible grin. 'No dear brother. I can kill you just as easily as I can let you live with your guilt. Do you understand?'

'Yes.'

'Good because I'm not like you. I won't kill you for wealth or power. If I kill you, it will be for a reason as old as hell itself, revenge. You don't know how much I wanted to kill the other seven. Watch them plead for their life like Lord Nichols did. He was fun. I sat on the side of the pool and watched Fido rip his head off and throw his body into the pool. The explosion of water and blood was absolutely breath-taking. But now it's your turn. The last of the Ten Lords. Once you die, I shall rule what's left.'

Martin watched as Sandra's grin disappeared. Her face took on an almost human air of indifference. She clicked her fingers, the amalgamated abomination by the stairs lumbered up from its crouch and worked its way across the roof.

Sandra's eyes met Martin's. 'You have two choices. You can run. Who knows, you might get far enough that Fido won't be able to sniff you out. Your second choice is a leap of faith. You can drag your mewling ass up off the floor and leap off of this roof. Maybe you'll live, maybe not. The choice is yours.'

Martin looked at his sister and then past her at the lumbering beast. He climbed to his feet and looked at Sandra. 'You don't have to do this,' he pleaded.

'I'm sorry, that's the wrong answer.'

Sandra glanced over her shoulder at Fido and nodded. The monster stood and cracked its interlinked fingers. Martin turned on the spot and sprinted for the far side of the roof. Sandra laughed as Fido sprang over her and closed the gap in seconds. The creature howled and swiped its claw through the air and across his preys' back. Martin stumbled and fell hard to the floor. Turning over, he kicked at the beast. A claw swung through the air inches from his face, red strips of torn flesh hanging from Fido's crooked nails.

Sandra snapped her fingers again. With a snort the monster clamped Martin's head in its mammoth claw and lifted him up. The beast took two steps towards the over the roof and dumped him on the edge. It released its grip and stepped back. Sandra skipped across the roof and jumped up onto the wall next to Martin.

'As much fun as this is, it's time to go. So what will it be? Do you want a head start? Run for your life, postpone the inevitable. Fido will catch you and tear you limb from limb, and then he'll stitch you back together so we can do it again.' She whispered in his ear. 'I'm going to enjoy this.'

Through teary eyes Martin looked at her, the grin was back, plastered across her face from ear to ear. Fido stepped closer and raised his claws. Martin turned to look out over the city and leapt.

The city exploded in a shower of fire and smoke. Towers of bone and flesh rocketed into the sky, hordes of the dead flowed over and around them. Rivers of pus and gore flowed down the sides of the towers and flooded the streets. Blood red clouds boiled across the sky, raining sulphur down on the remnants of the city.

'You know what; I didn't think he had it in him.' Sandra mused as she patted Fido on the head. 'But now the real fun starts.'

12days Of Christmas:2017

9. Ladies Dancing
Pippa Bailey

Crude chains scored the dusty ground, firing sparks across stone. An empty trunk covered in years of decay creaked open. Mildew fouled the air. Cobwebs furnished the red velvet interior, like intricate lace. Insects escaped the candle light, skittering thorough unseen holes. The trunk had lain barren for decades, a decadent reminder of finer times.

Two men dragged a large covered square, bound with rags and rope towards the chest, scraping through ancient detritus that coated the crypt floor. Covers tore loose, revealing a delicately painted foot smothered by flames. They lowered the hidden painting, its form skewed on the soft interior, and slammed the lid. Eruptions of dust danced in light.

Wincing under the bulky chains, they draped endless links around the chest, and hammered the final circlet in place. No one knew of this location, save themselves. Attempts to destroy the painting had failed. Fire licked at the canvas, caressing the figures, but would do no harm. Water neither. An ocean couldn't scour that paint, and dilute the power of those women.

They turned from the sealed chest, a multitude of bricks and mortar lay at their feet. Through solemn tears they sealed themselves inside, with any memory of this cursed painting. A slow burning candle, their only comfort.

It's unknown precisely when the initial symbol appeared, but the first incident took place in the autumn of 1832. A small half circle, a cross within its boundaries, smouldered on the curled bark of a birch tree, hunched along the church wall. Embers bore deep within the pristine lines, as if carved by a flaming knife.

A hazy Sunday afternoon, and noisy families poured from church doors onto cobbled streets. Children ran alongside their parents, kicking piles of rotting amber leaves. Reverend Bennett waved away his parishioners and toured the grounds. To any passer-by he was a joyful spectator, admiring families at play. A quaint pebbled path scored the outline of the church. He enjoyed his Sunday walks, soaking the last rays of autumn sun before winter descended. The twisted birch tree blotted sunlight, great roots clawed from the earth obscuring his path. The groundskeeper would need to tame this beast of a tree. He admired its mottled silver bark, running his hand against its roughness. The symbol called to him. His mouth twitched then hung slack. Transfixed, he drifted towards the tree, feet scored lines through soft earth. Eyes glazed, they drained of colour, until only orbs of white shuddering in damp sockets.

The symbol faded.

He launched back to the church entrance. His awkward gait covered ground quickly, scouring loose stones and mouldering detritus that tumbled alongside him. He shuffled to the raised pulpit and pressed his body against the cool surface.

CRUNCH. He slammed fists into the ancient wood. It splintered, plumes of dust filled the air and jagged chunks crashed at his feet. Oak slivers pierced his skin, blood pooling in torn flesh. Inside the breached space was a shining white square, a canvas. Untouched by decay, unnatural. Beauty amid dirt that clung to the jagged hole.

He grabbed the canvas, tucked it under his arm. Then stole away to his retirement room, sealing himself inside. He scrambled around on all fours. Books cascaded from shelves. Bottles struck each other, glass tinkling across stone, the floor showered in rich, floral, crimson. He clawed a dense mass of charcoal from the pungent fireplace ashes. It became his tool of choice.

Cross-legged, he scratched at the canvas. Black lines and marks formed undulating bodies. Nine women, nine wavering figures. He worked to exhaustion. Fingertips cracked, blood wept from open sores, droplets littered the canvas base. He worked until the charcoal ran out, until his fingers wore out. Scraping at canvas with nought but bloody bone stumps.

Fire gouged the cover of a nameless leather-bound book. Symbol two. It hissed, penetrating yellowed pages. A ream of coiled smoke infiltrated the confined office space, fouling the sweet smell of ageless books. A librarian rushed to the pile of returns, hunting the source. Books tumbled and slid onto the varnished floor. Acrid smoke continued to pour from atop the desk. She scrambled through the remaining stacks, and yanked the large tome from amid others. Her hands quivered, the book flapped in the air and clattered at her feet, pages spread. Curls of smoke snaked against her ankles, then vanished, drawn back inside the book.

A tendril of bitter drool slopped down Laura's chin. Red foam bubbled from her lips as she gnawed on them. Her eyes turned inwards. Muscles contorted, she crumpled to the floor, twitching.

Her colleagues rushed to the room, following the commotion, and struggled to help. Propped against the desk, her eyes twitched in a dream state.

Without warning, she leapt to her feet and palmed the desk top. Yanking draws open, she peered inside, shook her head and slammed them shut again. Pushing past her colleagues she staggered to the front counter, and swiped a pair of scissors.

She rushed though the entrance and onto the street.

"Where are you going?" they shouted after her, ignored.

Scissors clenched at her chest, she ambled to the church. Alnwick town was quiet in the early afternoon. Distant bells echoed, sound carrying on frozen wind. She barged the arched door, and stumbled along the pews to the retirement room. Forcing the door open, bottles scattered from where they lay, their outlines carved in dried wine.

Tap-tap-shhh. Reverend Bennett sat on the dirty ground. His flayed digits percussive on the charcoal figures. She placed a hand on his robed shoulder, acknowledging her presence with a twitch he peeled away from the canvas and left the room. His work was complete.

Beside the canvas lay a pristine ebony box, untouched by the chaos that had lain waste to the once lavish room. She admired the box, but did not yet touch it. Grabbing a chunk of hair, she pulled the lengths taught and carved at the bunch close to her reddening scalp. She dropped to her knees and shuffled towards the box. It clicked open as she drew close. Inside, a collection of paints. Immaculate crystal pots stowed a rainbow of colours.

She hiked up her many skirts, bare thighs prickled with goose-bumps from the cold room. Upturned pots dripped perfumed colour onto her naked skin. She blended with fingertips and rubbed at the flesh palette with her clumps of hair. Each stroke on the canvas precise, measured, perfect. Bloody charcoal women became flesh and warmth, seeming to shine from the canvas. A hue of pallid skin, lit by flames that crawled the floor. Living fire that licked their dancing feet.

Her brush of hair reduced with every stroke, individual paint soaked strands covered her clothes and stuck to her hands. She grabbed the scissors, cutting away another chunk, and began the process again.

Hours passed with every golden strand of hair cleaved from her scalp. Knotted piles littered the floor. A carpet of rainbow filaments surrounded her. Nine dancing ladies shimmered through wet paint. Their contorted bodies clad in a thin veil of white cloth, encircling a black form. They appeared to reach towards this central figure, this shadow of a man. Their effervescent glow drawn from him. Harvesting his soul, his essence.

She grated the scissor blades against her head. No more hair. Paint stuck her thighs together. Clambering to her feet, skin chaffed. She left the room. Spent.

Her hand twitched, scissors still poised against her scalp. Carving the symbol repeatedly into her tender flesh. Blood trickled into her eyes. People on the street screamed as she lurched from the church. Repetitive motion cleaving more skin from her skull. Many firm hands yanked the scissors from her grasp, and restrained her.

Charles pressed a warm cheek against the misty classroom window, tracing a symbol that corroded the frozen glass. It bubbled and oozed under his touch, like a batch of his mother's toffee. Crystalline tears wept onto the window frame and scorched his shirt, billowing harsh brown smoke.

Classroom empty, bar him. No one saw the glass melt and reform. No one saw him quiver, as if pummelled by electricity, or watched as he collapsed, his body a tangled mess. Thick foam leaked from his mouth, pooling on the dusty ground. Smoke spiralled from the crumbling embers of his shirt sleeve.

Playtime over, squawking children cascaded into the room.

Screams. Tears.

They yanked his fragile body and tried to wake him. Teachers ushered them to another room, and Charles was scooped from the floor by the headmaster. Prostrate on a desk, the school nurse got to work, whilst others ran to the doctor's surgery.

Singed fabric, cut from blistered skin. Nodules of corrupted yellow burst, leaking sticky fluid onto crisp white bandages.

Transported to the doctor's surgery in town. No explanation given for what had seared the boy's skin, or why he was unconscious. His eyes listed beneath scrunched eyelids. Angry parents blamed the school – a fruitless endeavour.

Tucked into rough cotton sheets, Charles shuddered in a fitful sleep. His parents taken to the doctor's office to discuss further treatment. Like a clockwork toy, freshly wound, he ticked and jolted. Sat up, eyes glazed. He leapt from the bed, opened the window and threw himself outside. An unseen force drawing him, like the others, to the church.

Darkness crept in, covering him in a thick blanket of shadow. No one noticed his buckling form stumble towards the church. Finding his way to the room with the canvas, he forced the creaking door to be met with the stench of sweat and wine. Feet stuck to mildewed red puddles and tumbled piles of colourful hair. Frozen before the painting's beauty he quivered, but did not move. The gaze of nine dancing ladies and their harvested man held him there.

Silent commands made him their puppet. Robotic, measured steps towards the ancient walls. This one blank, no shelves to obscure the stone. He smashed his face against the jagged grey, again and again. Blood seeped down his face, hot and sticky. It soaked into the remnants of his shirt.

Tiny fingers dabbed the streams of blood, and tapped crimson circles in layers. Minuscule fingerprints. Red flames licked beneath their dancing feet. Given a life of their own, stolen from that of a child.

Search parties scoured the darkness looking for him. Voices echoed around the church. His parents bellowed his name. Fear smothered them. He was not the first child to go missing in this town.

Fingers scraped gouges on his face. Thick oozing scabs, masked his forehead. CRUNCH... he threw himself against the wall. Wounds reopened, he worked fervently. Hours passed. His face no longer resembled that of the precocious little boy he was. Eyes sunken, slanted beneath torn flesh. Muscles weakened, his mouth a mere gash of broken teeth amid clawed lines of gore. His nose crushed, not the cute little button his mother adored, but twisted and gnarled like old vegetables, awash with red.

The painting complete, his blood ran dry.

Nine ethereal women. Their skin glowed from firelight at their feet. The centre of their convergence, a man of blood and ash. He had no form, no face. The women consumed him.

Charles turned his back on the painting and walked into the central body of the church. Crowds amassed on the pews, a vigil for the missing boy. She saw him, his mother. Identified by his burnt sleeve. Now with a face not even a mother could love.

"It's finished," he gurgled, lips sagging.

A chunk of torn skin sloughed from his forehead and slapped the floor. He stumbled towards his mother, and collapsed into her arms.

Days passed without incident. The painting's victims remained in a stupefied state. They babbled about the

Harvested Man, the nine dancing ladies, the nine circles of hell.

The symbol didn't appear again.

She floated above the surface of the ground. Mist beneath her pale toes ushered any debris from her path. Flowing locks of black hair writhed, suspended as if in water. She twisted and danced the alleyway, her thin veil of white fluttered in an unknown breeze. Seeking. Hunting.

A dishevelled man stumbled from a nearby tavern and vomited against the alley wall. He swiped chunks from his stubble with the back of his hand, and pushed himself off the wall with the other, struggling away from the effluent pool of his wasted earnings.

She watched.

The glow that emanated from her alabaster skin caught his gaze. Slack jawed, he hunched his shoulders, urging his uncoordinated body towards her. Transfixed, his senses dulled from drink.

Arms drooped to his sides. She floated closer. He could do naught but quiver on the spot. She circled him. Huntress and her prey. Fingertips caressed his body, stroked his long, matted hair. Broad chest exposed, she could see droplets of sweat form, tumbling southwards. Scorching palm against his trunk, she held him close. Her hand sizzled and slipped through his undamaged skin.

There was no discernible pain. Face blank, his chest heaved, panting. Her hand swam about inside him, skin rippled. She grimaced, withdrew her hand, and pressed her hot lips to his ear.

"Not the one," she whispered.

Fading, she skulked into the shadows, and was no more.

Possessed by a new urge, he staggered from the alleyway, his damp shirt flapped about him. The main road was dead, no illumination this time of night. Families tucked in their beds. No eyes to pry on the running man. He approached a small wooden sign propped outside a shop. Stopping, he almost admired the sign, its triangulated design. He slammed his body onto it, spearing his soft skin. Ripping, tearing him open. Glutinous intestines slopped onto the ground with a sickening thud. His dead weight forced the point through him, severing his spine. It protruded from mangled flesh.

The townsfolk found him, they couldn't understand his injuries. To have fallen with such force. A drunken tumble the only conclusion.

THUD.

Wooden splinters shot through the musky air and tangled in his beard. A long-handled axe wavered above his head, sunlight gleamed on its sharpened surface.

THUD. He let the axe drop again. A thick log split clean in half, chunks rocked on the dusty ground. He chucked the pieces into a dishevelled pile at the side of his crooked house. Fragrant sheets adorned the washing line, billowing like ancient sails. Leaves caught in autumn gusts buffeted the clean surface, leaving warped imprints from dirt and pollen.

Pine needles caught in tangles of blond hair and tumbled down her robed body. The woman twirled and danced towards him. Arms outstretched as if to draw him into her wavering rhythmical dance. Air heavy with a sickly-sweet stench. He retched and searched for the source. Slipping between sheets, axe dragged at his side, gouging chunks from supple earth.

Her approach, a sickness on the land. Nature silenced. Bird song muted, foul wind howled its last and cowered. Visage of a fallen angel, body as pale as the moon she too slipped between the sheets. Soft breasts swayed beneath transparent cloth that enveloped her delicate frame. Gormless, he reached for her. Silent laughter fell from crimson lips. She danced closer and circled him. Stroking fingers down his wiry chest, he gave in.

Attempting to hold her, she buckled and slammed a fiery hand against him, forcing undulating fingers under his taught skin. They moved like snakes, rippling under layers of muscle. His eyes rolled back, whites shining from his tanned face. A hushed moan acknowledged her exploration of his body. The axe shook in his hand, metal slamming against leather boots.

She pulled back empty handed. He twitched, and staggered forwards. She ignored his advances, and floated backwards through the fluttering linen.

"Not the one," she mouthed.

His chin slammed onto his chest, hand gripping the axe with renewed force.

CRUNCH.

He swung it up into his own shoulder.

Sharp metal sliced through his flesh like butter. Blood spurted from the wound, cascades of acrid iron showered the hanging sheets. He yanked it free, and swung again. Glinting silver cleaved flesh from bone. Blood showered his face, in pulsating bursts. His arm tore loose, skin split, tendrils of muscle flopping against his tattered shirt. It tumbled to the ground, fingers twitching.

Blood-loss slowed his progression, but he was still under her spell. Teeth grit, the blade struck his leg, splitting a hole in his trousers. Dry soil became pools of crimson mud. Bone splintered, and he collapsed to the ground, hacking at mutilated limbs.

His wife screamed when she found him. Her husband a mess of mutilated flesh; axe still swinging from his remaining arm.

There were more incidents of unusual deaths, mutilations, suicides. All men. Eight bodies in total.

The town was scared. A curfew placed to protect the people. God would protect them in their own homes, or at least that was the hope. Streets desolate after dark, save delivery men and animals that roamed the shadows.

The cursed figures were unrelenting. Any man who saw them destined to die.

Women claimed to have seen them, these dancing ladies. They called them witches, demons, women of the night. Dressed as angels to drag them to hell. A flash of white out of the corner of your eye. A figure dancing in darkness, slinking between shadow and light. The town's women kept their men home for fear they may lose them to the dancing ladies; the witch women of Alnwick.

Jasper had no woman to keep him home at night. No child to fret over. His work kept him on the streets at all hours.

It was dusk when he first saw her.

His post bag slammed against his leg as he left the office to start the evening round. A shadow flit across the ground, dancing with his own. He shook his head and continued to the first building. Three sharp knocks, no answer. He peered through the window, only darkness.

Peaches. He inhaled deeply, the air was sweet, unusually so. A white streak caught his eye. An undulating reflection rippled on glass as if it were water. A pale figure danced through the air behind him, arms grasping. He screwed his eyes and stared at the floor.

"Mustn't look…Can't hurt me if I don't look," he said under his breath.

He had always been a cautious man. Never one to take on a threat, he'd happily back down from a fight if it meant he'd keep himself safe. Avoiding danger cost him nothing. Bravery, he knew, cost lives.

The next address was two streets away. He walked with his head down. Rain filled holes from ancient lost cobblestones scarred the road. Pools reflected her shimmering mien. His eyes wandered, she was close.

He knew what had happened to the other men; men who saw the dancing ladies. Saw the stories in newspapers he'd delivered. Mutilations, drownings. One man hung himself in the town hall. Fear stole his breath, strangled him. His chest hurt from the vicious pounding of his heart.

So close, he could smell her. Hear the autumn air whip her robes against bare skin, like dove wings.

He ran. Cold tore at his face. He reached a grubby brick wall, and launched himself over. Scurrying into the doorway of a well-lit house, he waited. Skin crawling, like spiders –bristle legged, and twitching writhed beneath.

No woman. No sound. The door he leant against flew open and he tumbled inside. After a quick apology, a glass of water, and letters delivered, he begrudgingly left.

12days Of Christmas:2017

Unable to shake the feeling of being watched, he sprinted the rest of his route, eyes to the ground.

Tch-tch-tch. Tapping on his window pane woke him.

A sheet hung the length of his windows blocking moonlight. He'd never been able to afford a proper set of curtains, being a postman didn't pay very much. His mother had offered to make him some, but he never got around to taking her up on the offer. A dirty sheet had been draped over the rail. It did a meagre job, but was better than nothing.

Tch-tch-tch. He rose from his bed and approached the window in a daze. Brushing the sheet aside he peered out. Nothing. No branch colliding with glass. No bird having lost its way. He let the sheet drop, and collapsed on the bed. Air heavy with the scent of peaches went unnoticed. Eyes clamped, he didn't see the shadows grow, dance, slink across the floor towards his bed.

There were no footsteps as she danced across the room, toes scraping uneven wooden planks. She stuttered and vanished. Appearing again at the foot of his bed. Hands slid under the covers, elongating arms. They traversed his legs, longer, snaking towards his bare torso. Fingers crawled his body, the movement woke him. Black eyes, pitted voids peered from the end of the bed. He shrieked, stumbled onto the floor. Her puffy, white, tentacle-like arms burst from the covers and reached for him.

He scrambled to his feet and rushed down the stairs. Forcing the door, he burst out onto the moonlit street. Catching his breath, he stared up at his window. She stood, hands pressed against the pane. Shrunken arms, fingers protruding through the glass. He had seen her now, and knew she would take him, kill him, or make him kill himself.

He could run but she would find him. If she had tracked him back to his room, it wouldn't be long before she'd hunt him down and do whatever those women did to the others. This was a new fear. It scoured him from the inside, like broken glass teasing through his stomach. He felt sick, but starved at the same time, a gnawing ache. The unknown scared him so much more than the triviality of past fears.

He dodged between bowed willow trees lining a long stone path, that lead to rose gardens sat on the outskirts of the town. Beyond that Austin Albright's school.

Exhausted, he collapsed against a tree. Rough bark scratched bare skin. Jasper rubbed at the raw patches, before leaning back. There was an eerie stillness here. He could smell nothing but damp earth around him. The roar of blood in his ears, dulled to a throbbing babble.

Darkness called to him. He didn't know what time it was. Darting from his room, he'd left his watch behind. The moon was high, and stars seemed to blink at him though bleary eyes. He wrapped his arms around his knees, and buried his face. Snuffles of breath left clouds as he snored.

    Bird song woke him. He struggled to his feet, arm draped across his eyes to shade from the blinding sun. Arm wrenched around the tree trunk, he scoured the horizon for any sign of the woman. A low mist obscured his view. Spindly branches bent and warped. Fronds curled like charmed snakes, they weaved leaf strewn nooses that spiralled down and hung around him. He rubbed his eyes wishing the images away, and stumbled from the tree line.

    Ground shrouded in splinters of dead wood crunched underfoot. Trembling debris collided and tumbled along the earth. Crumbling rot hardened and shone like metal. Now taking the guise of curved blades that churned through fallen leaves. They dared him to walk the razors edge. His eyes stung from the pressure of his hands clamped over them. He ran blind, the scrape of gravel assured he remained on the trail.

    Years of trudging the same pathways, to walk them blind was little challenge to Jasper. He knew every pot hole, every street. A sharp left and a babble of voices signalled his destination. Lowering his hands, the light hurt. People stared and whispered. Who would listen to a dishevelled man running blind through the streets. He thought better than to ask for help.

He hammered the wonky brass bell on the police counter and expected them not to believe him. He hadn't expected laughter. Despite rumours, the police refused to accept anything was amiss. They'd heard it all before. Beautiful dancing women; they dismissed it as wild stories, no man had seen them before – none who'd lived to tell of it. And these multiple deaths, men at the end of their tether. Weak men. Cowards. These ethereal ladies a malady of the infirm women of Alnwick, and he should stop perpetuating the stories. Jasper knew different. Those deep dark voids, where eyes should be, still haunted him.

Slamming the door, he trudged home and ignored enquiring looks from people on the street. He peered inside, before entering. It was a mess, he wasn't sure it that was from his desperate attempt to escape in the dark, or from the woman.

He shuddered, remembering the sensation of her elongated arms. Spindly fingers crawling, like needle pronged insects that scuttled his vulnerable body. Reaching for his chest.

Hands plunged deep into desk draws, he fumbled for his knife. A small, but powerful blade. A gift from his father when he moved from their house, and into his own place above the post office. He flipped the blade around his fingers. Tiny movements, the knife twirled across his palm. A lifetime of quiet evenings and boredom afforded him the time to learn these skills. He stuffed it in his pocket, along with his watch, and collapsed on the bed.

He stared at the ceiling, and counted cobwebs that hung from dusty beams. He feared his eyes closing, knowing he'd see her again. If not in the flesh, then emblazoned on his eyelids. He had but a few hours until his next route was due.

Mind wandering, the ceiling blurred. Lines became a wash of white, thoughts meandered through empty streets. He imagined the route, feet sliding on smooth cobbles. Not chased, but something drawing him through mist smothered streets. Closer. He knew this part of town well, but couldn't pin point what summoned him.

Scraping woke him from the lucid dream. Eyes shifting to focus on the room. Blood fell in a steady rhythm and cascaded over his feet. His knife, bare blade gripped in his right hand, had sliced the skin from his palm. Symbols littered the aged door. A half-moon with a cross at its heart. Splinters, now red, sodden from fresh gore travelled in minute streams between cracked wooden planks.

He grabbed a sock from a draw and cinched his hand. Blood; first soaked cloth, then staunched. No memory of taking the knife from his pocket, or damaging the door. He ran a solitary finger over the scores. Intricate symbols. They held no meaning for him. He stood a while, afraid of himself. Scared of what these women had done to him. Finger-tips still caressing fouled wood.

BANG. BANG. BANG

Something smacked his door.

"Jasper! Where the hell are you? You should have been down here twenty minutes ago."

He slipped the knife back into his trousers.

Apologising through the door, he yanked on a shirt and struggled down the stairs into the post office side entrance.

He peered through the door to the front desk. A queue of package laden people shuffled on the spot. The letters he needed to collect were stored at the back of the building. He threw a satchel over his shoulder and wandered towards the delivery room.

It was silent here. Beyond the bustle of the desk, cart wheels crunching and floorboard creeks were the only sound. The room always thick with the vanillin musk of parchment and ink.

Jasper enjoyed the peace. It gave him time to think, much like his delivery routes. At one time he had wanted to be more than a postman, his room filled with notebooks and pages of poetry. He used to return home with new ideas. After multiple rejected submissions from the newspaper, he gave up. Accepted mediocrity, not that it didn't make him hate himself a little more every day. He still felt he was meant for more than this. Wanted to leave his mark on the world, to be more than a distant memory in years to come.

He scooted past desks strewn with forgotten packages, dust lining them like chalked bodies. Precariously stacked bundles of letters sat in a rack along the back wall. Indecipherable notes tacked below each cubby listed the streets. He stuffed crumpled envelope wads into his bag.

It wasn't apparent at first, the chill, the gentle breeze that carried in the familiar scent of peaches. His body tensed, heart in his throat. Shaking, he slipped a hand into his pocket, gripping his knife.

She shuddered into the room, twisting towards him in some music-less dance. The first time he truly laid eyes on her. Beautiful, porcelain skin, almost transparent. Clad in silken white, it flowed over her like spilt milk. Voids, a hollow eyeless stare bored into him. Coils of auburn hair weaved as though enchanted serpents, writhing behind her as she twisted and swirled. An elegant deathly approach. Bitter spit filled his mouth. Fear, nausea, he wasn't sure which clawed his throat raw. No door, no way out from this end of the room.

He lurched beneath a desk, scuffing his hands on the dirty floor. Hoping the desk would offer some protection before he could crawl to the door, he huddled against a leg.

She floated through the table. Cleaved in two, she spiralled towards him, parts moving independently, reforming like magnetic vapour.

He leapt from the table, knife in hand and slashed at her. The blade sunk into her cheek gouging chunks of pallid flesh. Beneath was oozing blackness. It shimmered and flowed like crude oil.

She shrieked.

Alarm bells rang, waves of sound struck him. He crumpled to his knees and covered his ears. Her keening tore paper from shelves, blasted packages from tables. Waves smacked him onto his back. He whacked his head on the floor, knocking him out.

Silence.

She trembled and stuttered, hands obscuring black fluid that trickled down her face. She vanished.

Voices in the dark woke him. Charles, Laura, and Reverend Bennett stood over him. Their disfigured bodies rank, putrid. Charles' eyelids drooped, sagging skin from his mutilated face weighing them down. Jasper screamed and kicked out, attempting to stand up. His head throbbed, his vision blurry. They didn't budge, just blankly watched his struggle.

"Get away from me!"

"The one," they chanted.

He pulled himself up on one of the tables, and teetered to the door. The post office was empty. Lights off.

"Hello?"

Nothing, save the chanting from the back room.

Outside, he sealed the door, grabbing anything to keep him upright.

The police station. He knew they hadn't believed him, but those three were real. Terrifying, but real. He'd heard stories about the librarian and Charles. Reverend

Bennett had been missing for two weeks. Retching, the stench of Bennett's putrescent fleshless fingers swirled in his mind. He hammered on the counter.

"Help! I need help!" He called into the darkness.

No police, no one around. He twitched, feet in constant motion, desperate for someone to hear him. Peering through the door to the cells beyond, three ethereal women writhed against each other, studying him. They disrobed, caressing supple skin, tempting him. He watched, transfixed.

CRASH. Noise brought him back from their hypnotic gaze. His pursuers burst from the post office and took to the street. He lurched down the road screaming for help, hunted by Charles and his cohorts.

He banged on doors. No one came to his aid. Not even a curtain fluttered, or window opened. The place was desolate.

Dancing ladies appeared from alleyways and doorways. Their shimmering forms writhed and twisted, disjointed movement slowing their progression.

He ran for the church. Hallowed ground would protect him.

Having never been much of a church goer, he wasn't sure what God would do for him, but he had to try.

Terrified, he crashed through the door, and threw himself down the aisle, past empty pews. Looking for a place to hide, he leapt to the back of the church. An arched door half hidden by tapestry would be his solace. Inside, he slammed the door behind him, sliding a desk and chair in front of it.

Lit candles covered the floor. He spun to look for somewhere to hide, a cupboard maybe. No such luck. A long dead fire, a few shelves of books, and an easel with a covered painting. At least he still had his knife.

The covered canvas drew him, almost forgetting the danger that lurked beyond the door. Curiosity got the better of him. He tore away the cover.

Nine beautiful dancing ladies – their movement almost seemed real. The nine circled around a shadow of a man. Reaching for him, his darkness a result of their light. At their feet, vivid flames licked upwards.

The painting was perfect, except one woman. Her face torn open, a gouge that scarred the painting. He knew that face, it was the one who came for him. The one he fought off, parting her pure skin, to reveal a sick darkness beneath. He tore a candle from the floor and held it to the canvas. It smouldered, flames lashed at the paintwork, but wouldn't burn.

BANG.

Someone slammed into the door. They'd found him. Tears swelled and carved paths down his face. Shaking, he held the flame against the women in the painting. Their faces charred. The paint bubbled and melted.

BANG.

Every candle extinguished at once, including the nub in his hand. Only a sliver of light remained, creeping in to the black room from the cracks in the door.

Shrieks rang from outside. He heard their chanting as they slammed against the door. Dust rained down from the small bolt that secured his safety.

Gripping his knife, he slashed at more pristine faces, destroying another two of the dancing ladies. The screams grew louder.

The blade began to quiver, he held it up to his face in disbelief, watching it vibrate in his hand. The metal buckled, sizzled, and folded on its self, melting into a stinking molten puddle at his feet. Shocked, he dropped the handle, which clattered on warped stone slabs.

BANG. BANG. BANG.

He scratched at the remaining faces with what little he had left of his fingernails. Tearing colour from the painting, until his nails broke and would do no more. He licked his fingers and rubbed at the paint on the last woman, smearing her beautiful face. He had done it. He'd destroyed the women, the torment had to stop.

THUMP.

They smashed through the door, destroying his makeshift defence, and leapt on him. His back cracked on the ground, bouncing and dragging his attackers with him. Loose bottles flew across the floor, glass cracked, drew blood, and chimed as it struck.

Stamping. Clawing. They tore at his body, and crushed his limbs beneath their feet. Skin split. Wounds widened, pulling flesh from bone. He pleaded with them, tried to push them away, but he was too broken, too weak. A flurry of finger nails tore through his chest and stomach. Skin flapped as their hands dove inside.

He screamed. Blood drowned the sound.

He managed to grab hold of Charles' leg and pull him to the floor. Reverend Bennett stomped on his arm. Slivers of bone pierced flesh, and stuck in the priest's boot. He reached down, gripping Jasper's marred arm at the wrist, and yanked it from the socket. Tender flesh gave way, an oozing pop resonated, and the arm was wrenched from his body. He flung the limb behind him knocking the easel, and sent the painting crashing down beside them. This was the end, he knew that. His body numb, heart thudding slowly in his ears. Sounding a death-knell.

Why hadn't it worked? Destroying the dancing ladies had done nothing. He could see the painting knocked onto its side next to him. The disfigured women held no power over him, over any of them. They never made it to the church. He made sure of that.

Blood loss made time slow. His attackers moved as if through water. He watched fleshless fingers tearing at his chest. His eyes wandered back to the painting.

There was the key, the shadow.

The harvested man.

With the last of his strength he ran his hand against the painting, smearing blood down the central figure, smudging the paint and obscuring him.

Jasper was gone.

They froze for a second, stopping their attack. Confused, they staggered away from the pile of flesh, blood and bone. Caked head to toe in gore, they fled, screaming for help.

Police collected the pieces of broken body, but were unable to identify the victim. After so many deaths in the two-week period, he was buried in an unmarked grave. His attackers were spared the noose, deemed insane, and committed.

The painting? That was never recovered.

"I'll turn this into a restoration room. Through here, the remaining crypt area will be emptied so we can have a dry store room for the gallery," said Mr M, pointing at the various named crypt stones that adorned the walls, each lined with a thick layer of cobwebs.

"It won't take much cleaning up, sir," said one of the architects, scribbling on a notepad.

Mr M tapped the head of his cane on the wall with a hollow thud. Ancient masonry crumbled to the floor, and showered them in dust. Coughing, they shone torch light through the hole. The architect shrieked and dropped the torch.

Mr M scowled, "Idiot. What did you do that for?"

He scooped up the torch. "There's bodies. Skeletons."

"What do you expect, we're in a fucking crypt. Shine that light back in there. I want a proper look."

Peering through, it revealed not a coffin, but another room. Light struck tarnished artefacts that hung on tainted walls. Crosses and small glass fragments were strewn about. In the centre a large dusty chest. Thick chains coddled its warped frame.

"So, what do we have here boys? Get it open!"

12days Of Christmas:2017

8. Maids Milking
Dani Brown

Somewhere in the fog they waited to grab at weary travellers. The guard advised not to use any lights and to stick together beyond the gate if they wanted to make it to the middle. The middle contained the mythical land of ideal presents for snobby in-laws.

Lisa had to get there. Being trapped in the in-between would be preferable to spending another Christmas listening to her mother-in-law moan about the wool-to-cashmere ratio in her scarf, carefully selected by Lisa in her favourite colour.

Lisa lacked the desire to impress, but she did want the woman to warm up to her, or, at the very least, shut up. The thought of another Christmas of Mitsy complaining about imaginary lumps in her mash made Lisa shudder. Mitsy wasn't even her real name. It made her sound like a porn star, but Lisa never mentioned that. Not worth the argument.

Mitsy really required a gag. That was her perfect gift. For Lisa.

It cost twenty gold pieces to get to the gate. There weren't any promises about passing through, or making it out alive. Everyone in the group had their own purposes for going.

The impoverished couple next to her scratched at their fleas and body lice. They could infest Lisa. She didn't mind, if she had the gift. Lice and fleas were a part of life. She had access to the best delousing creams.

Between scratches, the woman wiped at her eyes with her sleeve. The constant stream of tears cut through the dirt and left the skin raw. Lisa could only see the man's haunted eyes and stiff chin in the flickering torch light. The steady glow of mobile phones didn't work out there. She didn't want to think about how they acquired the gold pieces.

"The paths through to the other side shift."

A gasp sounded from the audience. Lisa turned her eyes back to the guard. Her heart raced inside her.

"Some are a trap to lure you to one of the Eight Maids. Understand they are rivals. They seldom team up. Use that to your advantage."

Forming an alliance with complete strangers had seemed better than facing another Christmas of Mitsy complaining when she paid her gold and booked passage into the dominion of the Eight Maids and onto the Land of Ideal Gifts. Every heart's desire waited.

Drones sent back about thirty seconds of white noise before going blank whenever they flew over the Eight Maids Dominion. The only stories circulating passed through the mouths of too many people to be reliable.

"I've been through once. It is forever night inside, but you'll set off in the morning. I'll lead you to the lodge. Spend the time learning each other's strengths and weaknesses."

Lisa followed the group into the guard house. She felt like they were being herded, ready for the slaughter. Her heart thumped in her chest and her mouth filled with invisible cotton. She wanted to be home with her husband and children.

The impoverished couple planted themselves in the corner. Their scarves looked like they had been tied around a tree – free to whoever claimed them, made using the spare bits of someone's yarn stash. Her own cashmere scarf suddenly felt too hot. It tightened around her neck, despite the loose way she tied it. She pulled at it with her fingers, still wrapped in matching gloves.

The other travellers dressed in a similar fashion to herself. The couple in the corner stuck out.

Lisa looked around the room. People looked at them, then looked down, heat rising on their cheeks.

She wondered what was in their sack. Looking around, she caught more than one set of eyes paused on it and knew she wasn't alone. The biggest comparable bags were the designer handbags weighing down the shoulders of the women in the room. Lisa didn't even know what hers contained beyond tissues, her purse and car keys hidden somewhere inside.

"There's not much talking happening. Introduce yourselves."

No one turned to look at the guard. Everyone was too busy trying not to look at the poor couple with the giant potato sack.

Lisa didn't like the way they scratched. It made her skin crawl.

"You two."

The guard pointed towards the couple, their infestations hidden by the shadows of the corner.

"What's your names? Why are you risking your lives? And the question these fine folk are too polite to ask, how did you raise the gold?"

The woman gasped and scratched at her head. Her hat's holes had obviously been repaired with different colour wools at different times. Lisa mentally slapped herself for judging. The couple already stood out, without the guard calling on them to speak first.

The bag dropped from the man's arms. The colour drained from his face with the thud. The woman groaned.

"Why such a heavy bag for a dangerous journey?"

The question didn't come from the guard, but from a woman to Lisa's left.

The man's eyes looked at the floor, as if he could burn a hole through it and escape. Lisa turned to see who asked the question.

"Yeah, what's in the bag?"

The room erupted in questions for the couple.

"Can you understand us?"

A woman stepped towards them.

"Yuck, fleas and that smell."

Neither stopped her from inching forward with her hand blocking her nose.

"You can pay for the debugging. You can afford to be here, you fix it."

Lisa felt the couple's humiliation vibrate through the floor and into her body, mixing with her own anxiety. The guard did nothing to stop the woman grabbing the sack, even when the man reached out his hand to stop her and the woman sobbed louder.

"What do you have in there, a dead body?"

The man went a shade of pale Lisa had never seen before.

"Steal the money to get here?"

The woman speaking looked at the shabby couple. They were a couple. There wasn't a ring, but the tender way in which the man pulled the woman towards him and sheltered her head and face in his chest gave it away.

"Ugh, what's leaking from it? Did you not think to invest in something waterproof? Oh wait," she paused to answer her own question, "you can't. Even if you could afford it, your fleas and body odour won't allow you into any shop and internet delivery doesn't arrive where you live."

The woman laughed. Light glittered on the man's face, reflecting the first sign of his tears. He reached again for the bag. The woman snatched it.

"Oh my god, it is an actual body."

She dumped it on the floor. Out tumbled the semi-decomposed body of a little girl. Lisa wanted to say she was five, but she was probably much older. The impoverished weren't known for their healthy eating habits and good life choices.

The woman stepped back. The room would have been silent if it weren't for the sobs of the couple in the darkened corner.

The body was bloated with gases and crawling with bugs. It appeared the skin breathed, even as the flesh rotted off. With part of her jaw visible, she had a double row of teeth. The adult teeth at the top, pushing down on the milk teeth at the bottom.

There was no mistaking the smell. On her trips into the slums, Lisa knew all the tricks so she wouldn't receive a big whiff of death.

"Guard! Guard!"

The woman who dumped the body onto the hardwood floor turned around. The guard buried his mouth and nose in a handkerchief with pink frilly edges while everyone stared at the body on the floor. Lisa amazed herself with her observation skills and wondered if it belonged to a wife or favourite mistress. She had been specially trained to notice everything under stress.

The guard heaved, swallowing his vomit.

"Guard!"

The woman stormed over and stood in front of him.

"I don't want them to join us."

Tears welled in his eyes. He mumbled beneath the handkerchief.

Lisa wanted to believe it belonged to a wife or sister. Her training being such a deep-rooted part of her instead said it belonged to a daughter he conned and manipulated his way into being granted custody so he could keep her under lock and key for his own sexual gratification. The part of her that believed the best of people hid beneath the scar tissue somewhere inside, far away from her team leader.

It would be too easy to claim the couple in the corner murdered their child through neglect and malnourishment and make it all their fault. They did the best they could by her, but society didn't like the underclass to raise healthy, well-adjusted children. It would lead to more competition for their own children.

"No one is phoning the police."

His voice cracked. The woman pulled a phone out of her bag. The guard took it from her hand.

High pitched laughter came from an open window. Suddenly, the chill of the night blew in from every crack in the building. The door crashed open and shattered into splinters.

A figure cloaked in silver floated into the room. Finger bones with skin dangling from them appeared out of a sleeve and pointed at the guard.

"Where's our payment, Jessop?"

Jessop forgot to swallow his sick. What he held in his mouth seeped out from beneath the handkerchief, turning the pink to a sickly shade of orange.

The creature hurt Lisa's eyes. When she looked away, her heart received the pain. Empathy looking for an escape from beneath the scar tissue. The man tried to put the girl back into the potato sack.

"What are you doing?"

Naked bones dangling dried skin pulled Lisa's hair off her neck to brush against the flesh there. The chills travelled from her spine throughout her body. She turned around to face her foe.

"You...you're one of the Eight Maids."

Lisa thought they couldn't pass the wall of decay that marked their dominion.

"I don't buy it," the woman who dumped the body shouted without waver in her voice.

She stepped forward and reached for the arm. The bones wrapped around her wrist. Her face went through motions of choking before she dropped to the floor dead.

"Where's our payment? You've been fleecing travellers. Send them into gawk at the Eight Maids without passing on their gold. That gold is their protection. We milk more than cows, you know."

Jessop looked like he wanted to faint. The impoverished woman did.

"Please, you're our only hope," the impoverished man shouted, jumping out from the corner.

"Jessop, the only way to help this man and his dear, departed child is our gold. Hand it over."

"I...I don't have it."

Lisa watched him swallow and wondered how much saliva it contained. She backed up. Suddenly, the guard house felt too small and hot, even with snow blowing in from the broken windows.

"Where do you think you are going?"

Finger bones grabbed Lisa's shoulders. The chill travelled through her coat and jumper to give her mind a flash of blackened flesh.

"I'm sorry."

"Room doesn't seem so hot now?"

"No."

"What's that? We can't hear you."

"No," Lisa repeated, this time with more conviction.

She stared straight ahead, looking at nothing. Icy breath clouded on her neck, making her wonder if icicles would form in her hair.

Lisa read up on the Eight Maids when she made the decision to get Mitsy a present she wouldn't complain about. Based on her research, she didn't think they could breathe. Air passed through them somehow to become even colder.

"Please, you have to help us. I'd do anything so my daughter can have a chance at life."

The man's reasons for finding the gold made Lisa self-conscious and shallow. Everyone else in the room would list reasons like her own, all except this man and his wife. The man commenced sobbing as if his tears could bring the dead back to the lands of the living.

"Where's the gold? The Heavens don't want to know what this man and his wife went through to raise theirs."

Jessop took a step back. Followed by another.

"Not so fast."

One of the Eight Milking Maids put her hands on his shoulder. Lisa tried to recall their names. She read so much information about them. The names were jumbled in their somewhere, dangling on the tip of her tongue.

"Our contract breached. Our dominion extended. And you are all standing in it."

The maid hissed, revealing her teeth sharpened into points.

Mouths contorted into screams, yet, no sounds came out. Everyone stood frozen. The impoverished couple ceased their sobs.

The maids circled Jessop, pushing people out of the way.

"What do we milk?"

The room was completely silent, even the wind stopped howling. Jessop swallowed.

"Innocent travellers."

Jessop looked down at his feet.

"We have a mountain constructed of gold. We don't have much use for it when we can simply take what we want."

The maid produced a gold coin from her pocket and bit it. When done, the maid flicked it at Jessop.

"We can't eat gold. The only people desperate enough to do business with us are middle-class travellers intent on impressing the neighbours."

Another maid joined her, flicking Jessop's ears on the way.

"The only people who deserve our help are them."

She pointed at the couple in the corner.

Lisa's mother-in-law cringed in her head.

I'm worth more. Get me something good. Satisfy my needs.

A maid turned to Lisa.

"We can read your thoughts, you know."

She grabbed her breasts, digging her icy nails in. Lisa felt warm blood beneath her undergarments.

"It wasn't so long ago we were milking beneath the warmth of the sun. A great enchantment banished us to the forest to rot away. The kindness of humanity flushed down the toilet and bleached by collective narcissism."

Lisa looked at her feet, too ashamed to stop the maid fondling her. The maid's rot entered Lisa through the cuts.

"There's kindness in you girl."

Heat rose to Lisa's face from her punctured breasts. In order not to end up like the couple in the corner, Lisa mastered hiding her compassion. She knew what she wanted. Fuck Mitsy, Christmas was about children since all religious observation had been banned under order of the ruling class. The couple's child deserved one last Christmas.

"Would you give us your mother-in-law instead?"

"In a heartbeat."

Lisa didn't need to think about it. Her husband would be sad but he'd get over it.

"What about yourself? Would you join us forever in our dominion so the child could be given life?"

Lisa thought of her own children. They needed their mother.

"We didn't think so," the maid spat.

She turned to the next person, leaving Lisa dazed. Blue fog crept into the building and circled around Lisa's ankles. No amount of cashmere-wool blends would keep the chill out. Mitsy's voice chimed in her ears. The words were difficult to make out at first, but Lisa knew they couldn't be saying anything pleasant.

Nothing here is good enough for me. Why waste your time? Your children don't need you. They need me.

The fog crept up Lisa's legs.

There is no place for kindness in this world. Do your last kind act. But, will it be kind? The child being dead is a mercy. The lower classes can't look after their kids. They breed like rabbits. They've got ten more at home.

Lisa slammed her hands to her ears and shook her head back and forth, drool flying from her lips. The fog danced around her hips. She needed to get out of there. Run. Run far away.

You aren't going anywhere.

Moisture from between her legs sent steam rising from her groin to mingle with the blue fog.

Look at that! Can't even control your bladder. My son is too good for you. My family doesn't want you around. Neither do my grandbabies. Don't run home. Run naked through the forest.

"You there," one of the maids shouted.

She pointed at Lisa, the voice of Mitsy was sent cowering to the deepest recesses of her mind. Lisa stepped forward, her coat hanging off her shoulders. She didn't recall unbuttoning it.

"What do you think you are doing?"

Lisa looked down. She couldn't see much through the blue fog. Her trousers were as unbuttoned as the coat. Mitsy was only a voice inside her head. She shouldn't hold any power.

As Lisa stood in the guard house, now part of the Eight Maids Dominion, she pictured her mother-in-law at home, twitching her curtains to spy on the neighbours. She buttoned her trousers. They were soaked with urine. No one would notice through the fog, except Lisa. The warm liquid turned cold upon hitting the air.

"We happen to like you. It isn't your fault the guard didn't pay us."

The statement made Mitsy's voice retreat further, slamming shut a door in her mind. Lisa pulled her coat up and buttoned it against the fog.

"Do you really want to get your mother-in-law a Christmas gift? Even if it was perfect and everything she ever wanted bundled into one package, it still wouldn't be good enough."

Hearing it spoken aloud made Lisa realise the truth in her worst fears. Nothing she could ever do would be good enough. She swallowed but didn't say anything in response.

"What would you like instead?"

She looked at the corner. She couldn't see the couple behind the blue fog.

"Are you sure?"

Lisa's mind drew a blank.

"What about the rest of you?"

Squeaks and cries sounded from all corners of the room.

"You wanted to come through our lands and take from us?"

"What was it you wanted that was important? As far as we can tell, only two people have a legitimate need to see us."

The room went quiet, except for the sobs of the couple in the corner.

I'm more important than anyone in this room.

Mitsy sounded muffled, as if she spoke through a closed door. Lisa supposed she did, one of her mother-in-law's making.

The couple over there, why should their child be brought back to die in poverty again? What good would it serve? There are too many of them in the slums already, fighting over scraps. Why give up your effort to shove the proverbial sock in my mouth with a decent gift, for once?

"Shut up," Lisa mumbled.

She shook her head. She couldn't see the eyes staring at her, but she felt them.

I didn't think you had enough self-respect to feel anything resembling embarrassment.

"Shut up," she said, this time louder.

Lisa heard the movement of people backing away from her.

"Hey, watch it."

"You're on my foot, stupid bitch."

You're the cause of all that. Look around. No one wants you.

Tears welled in her eyes. Mitsy wasn't whispering anything new. These were simple memories. Her husband dismissed his mother as joking and told Lisa to lighten up. The other women at the office reported similar stories to her own, with their own husband's dismissal. No one ever spoke of keeping the voice with them, hidden in their mind, to come out at times of stress.

You aren't going crazy. You already are. I told my son not to marry you.

"Lisa."

The voice of the maid drove Mitsy deeper inside, where she'd have to claw out.

"What do you want, for you?"

"I want her gone."

"How many women in this room can hear their mother-in-law, or maybe their own mother, scolding them in their heads? Be honest now."

No one said anything. The maids waited. Lisa didn't know how long for.

A woman screamed. A moment later that woman fell at Lisa's feet, the arm of a maid wrapped around her hair beneath the blue fog.

"This one has a story to tell. We can read it in her mind."

The woman cried, more dramatic than the couple in the corner.

"You're hurting me."

She made no effort to move. Lisa would have seen through the drifting fog. Lisa went to take a step back. Her feet couldn't move. It was like someone glued her to the spot.

The woman tugged at Lisa's trousers. When there was skin contact where the woman pulled them up a strange sound came out of Lisa's mouth.

"My mother-in-law punched me in the stomach when the abortion pills she slipped into my tea failed to work. She didn't want me having a baby. Bad genes, she said. The baby lived, but it is no life. I hate him. I hate her."

Lisa clutched at her mouth, unable to believe the words that came out.

"What is your business here," the maid asked.

"I want an undetectable poison. Not for my son, for the woman that did that to him."

The maid wrapped the woman's hair in her decayed wrist and threw her across the room, unwrapping it in one movement. She pulled another woman to Lisa's feet.

"What's your business here?"

The woman didn't speak. Again, the words came out of Lisa's mouth.

"I want to win the approval of my fiancé's mother."

"Everyone in this room knows that's never going to happen."

The woman was flung across the room.

"Please stop," Lisa said.

The fog seemed thinner, or it might have been Lisa's head. Dizziness swallowed her. She needed to sit down before she fainted.

"Seems everyone here is here to win the approval of someone else."

The maid turned to Lisa.

"Now, tell me Lisa, what would you like? Do you want the nagging voice to stop?"

Lisa shook her head yes. She turned to the corner and stopped suddenly. The fog lifted long enough to see both parents cradling the bag holding their daughter.

"If there was less approval seeking and less nagging mother-in-laws, do you think the world would be a better place? Less twitching of the net curtains to see what the neighbours have that you don't?"

Lisa shook her head.

"With less competition and more living for oneself, do you think that little girl might still be alive?"

There was movement in the corner of the room. Not from the couple.

"Where do you think you are going?"

A long arm reached out and grabbed Jessop. Lisa had forgotten about the guard.

"Why did you steal the money?"

The maid shook Jessop back and forth.

"Does it have anything to do with your own mother-in-law? You could walk into our dominion and take from the centre any time you want, why take the money?"

Jessop stared at his feet, or tried to, the fog was still thick around ankle height.

"What's that?"

The maid leaned in close. Lisa watched the horror spread across his face.

"Speak up."

"My mother-in-law…"

"Your mother-in-law what?"

"She...she spent all our money. Took a third mortgage. Took out a bunch of credit cards in our name. We'll be sent to the slums. I have children to feed."

"Once you're there, you can't get out, can you? Unless you have a visitor pass. Lisa could tell us more about that, but it seems pretty self-explanatory."

"You needed the gold because your mother-in-law worked up tons of debts? Whatever on?"

"I don't even know."

Jessop cried.

"This is what happens when me and my sisters are chased into the forest and locked up with enchantments."

Jessop looked up at them with tears in his eyes. They didn't show any pity.

"The world out there is falling apart around you and all you can think of is your fucking mother-in-law. The entire lot of you, except you two, in the corner."

The maid turned to the couple and knelt to their level. She whispered something too low for the other occupants of the room to hear. It stopped the couple's cries. They seemed brighter. Happier. They gathered their dead child and left through the parting blue fog without a word or look back.

"What did you say to them?"

"That is none of your concern."

A woman screamed as a maid grabbed her by the back of the neck.

"You know, these travellers have forgotten their fear."

The woman kicked. She didn't make contact with the maid holding her. The rest of the fog retreated. The light was brighter than before, Lisa had to shield her eyes. It was the only movement she could handle. With the maids occupied, it would be the perfect time to escape. They let the couple go, so they obviously didn't want everyone.

"We used to milk the souls of the living."

The maid holding the woman made sucking noises.

"People don't have much that would pass as a soul anymore."

Lisa looked at her feet. She knew the truth of the matter.

"Hey, that's not fair. Circumstances being what they are."

"Bad stuff happens to everyone, doesn't mean you need to pass it on to the next generation."

The fog crept back in.

"Our dominion has finally extended. We're in charge now. Leave this place."

No one in the guard house made any effort to move.

"Leave."

Leaving without my gift. I always knew you were weak.

"Shut up."

Lisa picked up her foot, heavier than usual, she slammed it back down again. It was the first foot movement she made in hours. It had pins and needles but she felt like she could try again. And she did.

Little steps aren't enough. They never were.

Cold, hard bone slapped across Lisa's face. Warm blood fell out of the cuts, burning her against the chill.

"We said to leave. You have a second chance."

Lisa took a step back.

Stay. I want my gift. It still won't be good enough, but that doesn't stop me from wanting it any less.

"Shut up you."

The mother-in-law that lived inside Lisa's head punched her grey bits. The maid in front of her slapped her at the same time, sending decayed flesh flying. Lisa watched it as it fell to the floor. Everything slowed down.

Lisa thought she heard the laughter of a child. The sound ended up distorted with the slow-motion engulfing everything, including herself. It could have been her mother-in-law, causing more damage inside her mind by biting the circuits. Mitsy was a biter. She hissed and growled too, like a cornered cat awaiting flea drops.

Lisa fought against the mother-in-law to shuffle backwards. Moving through the air was more like moving through glue. If she focused, she might be able to see the waves created when she dislodged particles to take their space.

The maid's looming face didn't get any further away. If Lisa watched closely, she could see the skin breathe. That might be how the undead survived because they didn't draw breath through decaying lungs. It would make the hiss of air she heard whenever one came close to her.

She shuffled backwards, each step putting up resistance and stared back at the face. Where the skin was left, it was blue, like the mist. She tried to look around. Moving her neck was too much effort.

The child's laughter sounded from outside again. Lisa snapped her head around, the slow-motion spell broken. She ran, feeling the eyes of the others in the room burning through her clothes and skin. Without Mitsy's voice screaming in her head, she felt lighter.

She ran through the shattered remains of the door and into the cold air outside. Dirty snow fell from the sky. She didn't bother pulling up her hood. The holes through her coat and jumper let the cold air press against her skin. She found it refreshing after being cooped up with the decay.

Lisa ran towards the path and the sound of the child. She heard the guard house behind her. She wasn't sure if the Eight Maids would let anyone else go, or how far their new territory expanded. It didn't matter, she was free. She was free to consider ways in which to deal with her mother-in-law and a career change.

She caught up to the impoverished couple. Their child skipped between them, laughing. They seemed richer than the rest of the group put together as Lisa ran past them, looking back. The mother gave a wave, as did the father.

The child ran up to Lisa and held her hand. Lisa didn't feel her flesh crawl as she did on so many trips into the slums. Instead, a warmth embraced her, even as the trees held her within their circle of blue fog and decay.

Another refugee from the guard house caught up and ran straight past them into the wall of trees. There wasn't a break or any way to scale it. The little girl's laughter echoed all around them, bouncing off the forest.

Lisa looked down. The girl wasn't any less decayed than she was when she fell out of the bag. She pulled off her own gloves to inspect her hands. No blood ran through them. What had been in her, leaked into her undergarments and dried to her chest.

The child pulled her around the perimeter to a gate. Muffled voices spoke from behind it. Lisa could just about make them out.

"Do not separate from the group."

"I've come here for one reason and one only. If no one will help me, I'll go it alone."

Lisa heard her husband's voice above the guard.

"Daddy, is mummy in there?"

Her dead heart fell.

7. Swans A Swimming

G. H. Finn

With original text from (and apologies to) Joseph Jacobs (1854-1916)

On the seventh day of Christmas...

After hours of watching the traditional TV reruns of James Bond films , The Sound of Music, The Great Escape and The Wizard Of Oz, all while playing with expensive presents that were already beginning to seem rather dull, the day was finally over.

It was now the seventh night of the Christmas holidays, better known as New Year's Eve. And it was time for the children to go to bed. Whether they liked it or not.

Of course, they didn't like it one little bit.

Janet and John, the Grimbold twins, were well educated to the point of erudite precociousness (they had been forced to learn to read at a very early age, something their parents had later come to regret). The pair of siblings were now worldly-wise well beyond their thirteen years and unhesitatingly outspoken when stating their opinions. Or, as Mr Grimbold put it, "They're a right pair of arrogant, annoying little brats".

The children had determinedly wanted to stay up until midnight to see the New Year in with their parents. They were told in no uncertain terms that this was not going to happen, despite the twins whines and wails of protest. Mr and Mrs Grimbold had other plans. Mostly involving champagne, vodka , whiskey and cigars. Mrs Grimbold liked a good HavavaHavana, much to her husband's annoyance. But he shrugged, it was the turn of the year after all. They were going to a party at Mr Grimbold's golf club. Adults only. And the children would have to lump it.

The Grimbolds had been worried they wouldn't be able to find a babysitter on New Year's Eve. But they were in luck. Old Mrs Cygnus, who lived down near the lake, hadn't had any plans for the evening and she'd agreed to look after John and Janet. The waddling old lady, swathed in downy waves of white hair, wasn't exactly the children's favourite person. John said she looked like an old witch. Janet said she was ugly. Mrs Grimbold had scolded them both for that, telling the pair that Odette Cygnus was a very nice old lady and that they shouldn't judge by appearances. "Remember the story of The Ugly Duckling!" she'd said to her complaining children. John had turned to Janet and whispered, "If we're going to remember fairytales, Hansel and Gretel is the one that comes to my mind... But she's too fat for us to shove her in the overoven." Janet laughed under her breath, a wicked grin on her pretty young face.

Mrs Cygnus arrived and the Grimbolds swiftly left. Reluctantly, an hour after their agreed ten o'clock bedtime, the children eventually went upstairs amid a chorus of grumbles. The old woman did her best to be nice. To the twins' horror, she tucked them both into bed and offered to read them a story.

"Does she think we're five-year-olds?" muttered Janet to John, not quite under her breath.

Mrs Cygnus had brought an old, worn-looking book with her. John read the title in disgust and rolled his eyes at Janet. She glanced at the book and grimaced, silently mouthing the words "Fucking Fairy Stories".

The elderly woman propped herself in a chair and opened the book, saying, "Joseph Jacobs' versions of folk tales aren't exactly very accurate, but you might like this one. It's called The Swan Maidens." With that, she She settled back, dispensed with the traditional 'Once Upon A Time', and immediately began to read.

"There was once a hunter who used often to spend the whole night stalking the deer or setting traps for game. Now it happened one night that he was watching in a clump of bushes near the lake for some wild ducks that he wished to trap. Suddenly he heard, high up in the air, a whirring of wings and thought the ducks were coming; and he strung his bow and got ready his arrows.

But instead of ducks there appeared seven maidens all clad in robes made of feathers, and they alighted on the banks of the lake, and taking off their robes plunged into the waters and bathed and sported in the lake. They were all beautiful, but of them all the youngest and smallest pleased most the hunter's eye, and he crept forward from the bushes and seized her dress of plumage and took it back with him into the bushes."

"He sounds like a right peado,." said Janet.

"A rapist for sure,." said John.

Mrs Cygnus either didn't hear the children or chose to ignore them and continued,

"After the swan maidens had bathed and sported to their heart's delight, they came back to the bank wishing to put on their feather robes again; and the six eldest found theirs, but the youngest could not find hers. They searched and they searched until at last the dawn began to appear, and the six sisters called out to her, "We must away; 'tis the dawn; you meet your fate whatever it be."

And with that they donned their robes and flew away, and away, and away."

"What a bunch of heartless bitches!" opined Janet.

"You're not kidding," said her brother, "Leave their now naked youngest sister alone in the woods? I can imagine what Social Services would say about that. She'd be taken into care before you can blink.,"

The old lady readspoke a little louder, reading,

"When the hunter saw them fly away he came forward with the feather robe in his hand; and the swan maiden begged and begged that he would give her back her robe. He gave her his cloak but would not give her theher robe, feeling that she would fly away. And he made her promise to marry him, and took her home, and hid her feather robe where she could not find it. So they were married and lived happily together and had two fine children, a boy and a girl, who grew up strong and beautiful; and their mother loved them with all her heart."

"So no just a paedo and a rapist, but a thief as well,." said John.

"Add to that forcing her into a marriage against her will? The heartless misogynist bastard," said Janet. "Does that come under 'human trafficking' or 'unlawful imprisonment'? I'm not sure."

Mrs Cygnus took a deep breath, then said,

"One day her little daughter was playing at hide-and-seek with her brother, and she went behind the wainscoting to hide herself, and found there a robe all made of feathers, and took it to her mother. As soon as she saw it she put it on and said to her daughter, "Tell father that if he wishes to see me again he must find me in the Land East o' the Sun and West o' the Moon;" and with that she flew away."

"That probably counts as 'abandonment' and 'neglect' on the mother's part,." said John, knowingly.

"Yeah, but they'd never get a conviction," said Janet, "She could plead diminished responsibility due to being forced into marriage and having two kids by her thieving, kidnapping, rapist husband."

"Fair point,." John admitted.

Mrs Cygnus took a deep breath and continued, spoke a little louder, continuing.,

"When the hunter came home next morning his little daughter told him what had happened and what her mother said. So he set out to find his wife in the

Land East o' the Sun and West o' the Moon. And he wandered for many days until he came across an old man who had fallen on the ground, and he lifted him up and helped him to a seat and tended him until he felt better."

"You've got to admit that whatever she'd been through, that girl was as thick as shit leaving instructions for her husband on where to find her. She should have gone to a women's refuge or something," tutted Janet. "And who'se looking after the two kids now?"

"I'm not sure about this old man who'd 'fallen to the ground' so conveniently," said John. "Sounds like the next line should be, 'Honestly, he was already laying here like this when I found him, officer.' We already know he's a thieving sod. Probably a dirty mugger too."

Janet nodded and the babysitter read on,

"Then the old man asked him what he was doing and where he was going. And he told him all about the swan maidens and his wife, and he asked the old man if he had heard of the Land East o' the Sun and West o' the Moon.

And the old man said, "No, but I can ask."

Then he uttered a shrill whistle and soon all the plain in front of them was filled with all of the beasts of the world, for the old man was no less than the King of the Beasts.

And he called out to them, "Who is there here that knows where the Land is East o' the Sun and West o' the Moon?" But none of the beasts knew.

Then the old man said to the hunter, "You must go seek my brother who is the King of the Birds," and told him how to find his brother."

"Sounds to me as though all these guys are in some kind of secret sex ring, the Daily Mail is always going on about them," said John, "I mean, the poor swan girl runs away and all of a sudden mysterious men who only meet each other as strangers in the woods are falling over themselves to help find her... Suspicious to say the least."

His sister nodded. "King of the Beasts?" said Janet, "Who does he think he is? Alastair Crowley? King of the Beasts my arse. More like King of the Doggers."

Mrs Cygnus might possibly have ground her teeth but it was hard to tell as she carried on reading without a pause,

"And after a time he found the King of the Birds, and told him what he wanted. So the King of the Birds whistled loud and shrill, and soon the sky was darkened with all the birds of the air, who came around him. Then he asked, "Which of you knows where is the Land East o' the Sun and West o' the Moon?"

And none answered, and the King of the Birds said, "Then you must consult my brother the King of the Fishes," and he told him how to find him."

"I told you! It's a sex ring!" said John, gleefully. "Their using aliases and code names. The first guy in the woods is the King of Bestiality, his 'brother' is in charge of procuring all the 'birds' and the third guy dresses them in fish-net stockings before they pimp them out."

"Makes sense,." agreed Janet.

The old woman raised her voice again, reading swiftly and loudly to drown out any interruptions,

"And the hunter went on, and he went on, and he went on, until he came to the King of the Fishes, and he told him what he wanted. And the King of the Fishes went to the shore of the sea and summoned all the fishes of the sea. And when they came around him he called out, "Which of you knows where is the Land East o' the Sun and West o' the Moon?"

And none of them answered, until at last a dolphin that had come late called out, "I have heard that at the top of the Crystal Mountain lies the Land East o' the Sun and West o' the Moon; but how to get there I know not save that it is near the Wild Forest."

So the hunter thanked the King of the Fishes and went to the Wild Forest. And as he got near there he found two men quarrelling, and as he came near they came towards him and asked him to settle their dispute.

"Now what is it?" said the hunter.

"Our father has just died and he has left but two things, this cap which, whenever you wear it, nobody can see you, and these shoes, which will carry you through the air to whatever place you will. Now I being the elder claim the right of choice, which of these two I shall have; and he declares that, as the younger, he has the right to the shoes. Which do you think is right?"

So the hunter thought and thought, and at last he said, "It is difficult to decide, but the best thing I can think of is for you to race from here to that tree yonder, and whoever gets back to me first I will hand him either the shoes or the cap, whichever he wishes."

So he took the shoes in one hand and the cap in the other, and waited until they had started off running towards the tree. And as soon as they had started running towards the tree he put on the shoes of swiftness and placed the invisible cap on his head and wished himself in the Land East o' the Sun and West o' the Moon. And he flew, and he flew, and he flew, over seven Bends, and seven Glens, and seven Mountain Moors, until at last he came to the Crystal Mountain. And on the top of that, as the dolphin had said, there was the Land East o' the Sun and West o' the Moon."

Out of breath, Mrs Cygnus paused.

"Thieving bastard!" said Janet.

"Typical conman, always hustling and robbing the marks," agreed John, adding, "But they were total numbskulls to ever trust him."

"Too true,." agreed Janet.

Mrs Cygnus cleared her throat and read on,

"Now when he got there he took off his invisible cap and shoes of swiftness and asked who ruled over the Land; and he was told that there was a king who had seven daughters who dressed in swans' feathers and flew wherever they wished.

Then the hunter knew that he had come to the Land of his wife. And he went boldly to the king and said, "Hail, oh king, I have come to seek my wife."

And the king said, "Who is she?"

And the hunter said, "Your youngest daughter." Then he told him how he had won her."

"Won her? Won her?" exclaimed Janet, "He sees a young girl in the woods, steals her clothes, refuses to give them back, makes her his sex-slave with a sham marriage and calls that winning her?"

John nodded, "And if I were her Dad, I'd probably have a few stern words to say to my other six daughters about leaving their youngest sibling to wander naked in a forest too." he added.

The old babysitter pressed on with the story,

"Then the king said, "If you can tell her from her sisters then I know that what you say is true." And he summoned his seven daughters to him, and there they all were, dressed in their robes of feathers and looking each like all the rest.

So the hunter said, "If I may take each of them by the hand I will surely know my wife"; for when she had dwelt with him she had sewn the little shifts and dresses of her children, and the forefinger of her right hand had the marks of the needle."

"Oh, this just gets worse," said Janet, shaking her head. "The Dad is clearly part of the whole sex-ring. And as for the so-called husband… He's had two children with his 'wife' yet can't even tell her apart from her sisters? He obviously didn't spend much time looking at her face. He probably had a bag over her head the whole time."

"Not just that," said John, "But this whole story about pricking herself while sewing clothes for the children sounds very fishy to me. Basically he's saying he'll be able to recognise her because of the needle-marks on her arm. He's obviously had her on smack to keep her docile."

The white-haired old woman coughed and said loudly,

"And when he had taken the hand of each of the swan maidens he soon found which was his wife and claimed her for his own. Then the king gave them great gifts and sent them by a sure way down the Crystal Mountain.

And after a while they reached home, and lived happily together ever afterwards."

"Crystal Mountain? Sounds like some polite euphemism for Meth," muttered John.

"Is that it?" asked Janet in disbelief, "That's the end of the story? Her Dad gives the kidnapping, thieving, rapist, drug-pushing conman some presents and sends his daughter off to live with the bastard?"

Mrs Cygnus closed the book of fairy tales and looked at the children clearly, her eyes twinkling in the darkened bedroom. "I did say that Joseph Jacobs' version of the story wasn't very accurate..." she said softly.

"Oh yeah?" asked John, "And I suppose you know what really happened do you?"

Janet sniggered.

Mrs Cygnus smiled an enigmatic smile. "Perhaps I do. Would you like to know the true story of the seven swan maidens? The original story. Before it became distorted, filled with lies. The old version from long and long ago? From way, way, way before the Victorians sanitised it for the benefit of innocent, unsullied children such as yourselves?"

The children sat up in bed. This was more like it.

"Tell us!" said Janet eagerly.

With a sigh, the old woman settled back into the armchair and in a dreamy voice, heavy with the burden of years and the greater weight of memory, she began.

"Once, far ago and long away from here, in a time that was not a time, in a place that was not a place, it was deep night in the most ancient of forests.

It was cold. Very cold. Oh so very cold. Dark. Very, very dark. Blacker than chimney soot. Blacker than the bleak midwinter midnight. Darker than the heart of a thrice-burnt witch.

Seven sisters flew fleetly through the star-strewn sky, flying to the lake, wide awake and dreaming in that silent night. Feathers fluttered softly, falling down as they shed their long white cloaks among the oaks, bare in the wicked winter chill. Mute, they waded into water, daughters of Lir, the king.

Seven swans swam in the dark silvered lake.

Lusty eyes watched them, hidden, unseen between evergreen branches.

The shepherd should have been watching his flock that night, but he abandoned his sheep to peep at the maidens. He had heard the tales. He knew they would come to swim, naked in the black and silver lake. Swan-girls. Carelessly at home in those waters that no man would enter, for fear of being dragged down. Down among the drowned.

He stalked them. He crept. Creep, creep, creep, when he should have been asleep , sleep, sleeping. . Prying, spying, eyeing the swan-maids. He found their cloaks of white feathers, cast off upon the heathers, hung on holly bushes, and then as a bull rushes madly, he gladly grabbed one cloak, and slunk away, drunk with success, careless of the distress he'd cause to an undressed maiden. Laden with his feather-light prize, his eyes, as before, watched once more, while seven swan sisters swam ashore.

Six sisters swiftly dressed, pressing their pale wet breasts into tight, feather-bright robes.

One sister stood alone. White as bone. Uncloaked. Water dripping from her wet hair.

Her silent sisters smiled at her, winking. And in the blinking of an eye they were gone from sight, in flight, away among the shrouding clouds.

One swan-sister. Left behind. On her own. Alone.

Alone but for the ever watching eyes.

He stepped out, boldly. Coldly eyeing her. Hungrily.

He held out her cloak, mocking her, shocking her with his cruel smile.

He thought her helpless. Flight stolen from her.

She smiled. Mutely she beckoned to him, and forth he came, eager to embrace her, calling her his "True Love" and laughing that he had a "Gift" to give her."

Old Odette Cygnus paused, as though remembering. She smiled. It was not a pleasant sight. With her eyes shining in the darkened bedroom, she continued her story.

"No true lover he, and I knew what he would have given me.

They say a swan can break a man's arm. I broke his.

12days Of Christmas:2017

My first fist flew, like a wing, swinging swift and true, flying to fracture his oh so brittle bone. Skeleton fragments of red and white blossomed in the night, piercing his frail fragile flesh. No clean break this, but a shattering, with shards shearing through his arm, to leave him harmed and harmless, bleeding, broken upon the eggshell shore. Yet I was not done, having only just begun. First one arm, then the other.

Next I broke his legs.

He would have cried aloud in his rage and pain, but, to silence him, I had torn out his tongue by its root. Mute, his blood fountained forth from out of his red raw mouth. Dumb and shattered he shuddered and spluttered a wordless swan song.

With a smile I carried the man gently into the waters, summoning my cygnet siblings.

Seven sisters together, we took him to the centre of the old, old, old dark lake and circled him, watching merrily as he struggled to swim with broken limbs. Joyfully we offered him to our mother, She Who Dwells Within The Lake.

As a parting gift to the sacrifice, we let him see the watery ripples around our nipples while he drowned. Gurgling. Gargling with water and blood.

And then, all was once more silent on the darkly silvered waters of swan lake.

No sound disturbed the night as seven silent swan sisters swam cheerily above the rotting bones of men."

"Now hush my little chicks," said Mrs Cygnus to the silent children, pale and shivering, hiding beneath their bed-clothes.

"Settle in your nest. It is time for you to close your eyes. And sleep."

The room was filled with the sound of feathers fluttering as huge wings stretched, and the old woman whispered.

"Rest in peace my pretty ones. Sleep well. Sleep sweetly in the long, bleak midwinter darkness in that deep and silent sleep, who knows what dreams may come?", for in that in that deep and silent sleep, who knows what dreams may come?

6. Geese Laying
Mark Leney

When Old Mister Andersen brought the first golden egg to be valued at Reggie's Pawn Brokers, the proprietor, Reginald "Reggie" Thompson had thought it to be a one-off, never to be repeated event.

On that day, Reggie had examined the egg through his special lens. There had been no denying its authenticity and the pawn broker had readily agreed to pay Mister Andersen the true monetary value of the egg. It had been worth just over £250 in all. Reggie had sold the egg to a jeweller where it could be melted down and turned into jewellery with a £50 finder's fee on top of the original £250 value. It had been one of the most lucrative acquisitions in all of Reggie's fifteen years in the pawn broker's business.

And so, you can imagine his surprise when Old Mister Andersen returned the following month with three more eggs identical in every way to the original. Once again Reggie was willing to write this off as another one-time deal. Perhaps the old man had a collection of these golden eggs and was just selling them as and when he needed to. This is what he told himself the third time around and even the fourth. It was only after Old Mister Andersen's fifth visit that he began to suspect something else might be up.

On that fifth occasion the old man brought three eggs. He never brought more than three. This time Reggie decided that he would ask Old Mister Andersen just where he was getting these golden eggs from.

"This must be quite a collection of golden eggs that you have, Mr Andersen." Reggie stated in a conversational manner. "I can't say as I've come across the craftsmanship before. All of them virtually identical. Who makes them, do you know?"

Old Mister Andersen chuckled in good humour and offered the pawn broker a conspiratorial wink.

"It's an old family secret, Mr Thompson!" he answered quietly. "If I told you I'd have to kill you. I'd say that you could ask the last man I told, but sadly he's no longer with us."

Reggie laughed along with the old man's little jape.

"Very funny, Mr Andersen. But my business operates on strict confidentiality. You can tell me," he insisted.

"Yes. That's what the last one said," again with that chuckle. Reggie thought that he detected a sinister undertone to the otherwise cheerful sound. He shook his head dismissively. There was nothing sinister about Mr Andersen.

In that moment as he concluded his business with the old man, Reggie decided that he would follow Old Mister Andersen home and discover just what the secret of the golden eggs was.

After the old man had left his shop, Reggie spied on him surreptitiously through the window, giving him enough of a head start. Once he felt that he'd waited long enough Reggie flipped the 'closed' sign into view on the front door and then exited onto the cobbled street outside, stopping only to securely lock his livelihood before taking off after Old Mister Andersen with as much stealth and guile as he could muster. He'd taken the time to slip into a crumpled beige Macintosh coat and a trilby hat sat upon his head; the collar of the coat was turned up and the hat was tilted to allow Reggie the delusion of anonymity as he tailed the old man back to his abode, but as he scurried along the slick, rain soaked streets, occasionally ducking behind parked cars or into alleyways should the old man ever chance to look over his shoulder, he more resembled a grubby parody of one of those clichéd Film Noir private detectives that were immortalised in movies and pulp novels back in the 1930s. All that was missing was the inner monologue.

Reggie's thoughts were a long way away from monologing. He was too busy speculating on what Old Mister Andersen's secret might be. Could it be a collection of heirlooms? Did he somehow make these eggs himself? If so then why not sell them as ornaments? Why take them to a pawn broker?

As these thoughts ran through Reggie's head he was forced to endure what must be the old man's routine every time he came into town as he observed him going in and out of other shops.

He saw him go into the betting shop and the butchers, where he observed the old man by some gorgeous looking steaks and sausages. There was a trip around the local supermarket and before that Reggie had to exercise his patience as he waited for Old Mister Andersen to get a haircut at one of the local barbers.

Finally, after a glance at his watch told Reggie it was six o'clock and the pawn broker cursed himself for all the business that he'd missed out on for closing early, Old Mister Andersen made his way to a bus stop and waited with his new haircut and his shopping for the bus that would carry him home.

Reggie realised that he would have to take the same bus as the old man if he was to follow him to where he lived. He had been a fool not to anticipate this. Reggie turned up his collar that little bit further, sinking his head into his shoulders and tilting his hat forward as he lingered at the back of the bus stop in an effort not to be recognised. Fortunately, the old man seemed too wrapped up in his own little world to notice too much about who or what was going on around him.

Soon, the bus pulled up at the stop and Old Mister Andersen clambered aboard. Reggie listened out for the stop that the old man asked for as he paid for his ticket and made sure to ask for the same as he bought his own then he made his way, head down inside his collar, to the back of the bus and sat down to wait for them to arrive at their final destination.

The bus ride took about half an hour and Reggie had to fight off the urge to fall asleep as the vehicle rattled along its route. Every bump and pothole that the bus hit served as an aid to jolt Reggie awake, yet at other times the rocking of the vehicle acted like a baby's cradle and exacerbated his efforts to remain alert.

Eventually he spotted the old man pressing the buzzer for his stop. The bus slowed down to a halt at Mr Andersen's required destination and the old man hobbled off gradually with his shopping. Reggie hung back as far as he could before stepping off the bus to continue his stalking.

Old Mister Andersen remained apparently oblivious to the 'shadow' that lurked behind him, latched on as firmly as chewing gum on the bottom of a size 10 boot. Reggie ducked down behind a stationary Robin Reliant as his quarry finally turned onto the pathway of what was presumably his house. The pawn broker watched as the old man set down his shopping bag and pulled out his keys from an inner jacket pocket. Once he had unlocked his front door Mr Andersen picked up his bags once more and stepped inside.

Reggie watched the front door slam shut from his hiding place. Certain that he was safe from detection, Reggie stood up from behind the parked car and tried to think on how he should proceed. Should he go and knock on the front door? And say what exactly? Maybe he could force his way in once the door was open and 'persuade' the old man to reveal his secret?

No, Reggie didn't find that palatable at all. He wasn't a thug or a criminal. He was just curious.

It was then that he heard what sounded like the honking of geese from the back of the house.

Reggie was no ornithologist, but he knew what geese sounded like. His mind wandered back onto the golden eggs.

"Nah" he murmured out loud. "It can't be."

Nevertheless, he made up his mind there and then to try and get a look at the back of the house.

Unfortunately, Old Mister Andersen's home was a terraced house locked between two other houses and there was no side passageway that led through to the back.

Reggie realised that he was going to have to walk to the end of the street and go down the alley at the back of the houses. This he did, muttering obscenities under his breath as he went.

Now that the sun had gone down it was noticeably colder and Reggie was thankful that the trench coat and hat that he'd initially worn as a disguise was now serving to keep at least some of the chilly evening air at bay.

Reggie turned into the alley. It was rather dark. Anything or anyone could be lurking in the shadows, waiting to pounce and with only one or two street lights dotted along the walkway to provide splashes of illumination in the sea of darkness that loomed before him it almost gave Reggie pause to turn back and give up on this venture. But not quite.

He walked down the alley as quickly as he could and almost fell flat on his face as he caught his foot upon something that lay unseen in the shadows. Reggie steadied himself by reaching out a hand to touch the fence. Looking down he saw that some prat had dumped a dirty old, moth-eaten mattress on the ground outside the door to their back yard.

Reggie cursed the former owner of the mattress as he stepped over it and continued down the alley. He had counted the houses as he had walked down the street so that he would know when he got to the back of Old Mister Andersen's house and he counted now as he picked his way through the darkness. As he got closer though he heard the calls of the geese again and it didn't take long for him to single out the back yard that he needed.

Now that he was standing at of the back entrance of Old Mister Andersen's yard Reggie found himself wondering just how he was going to get inside. He tried the gate on the off chance that it would be unlocked. It was so stiff that Reggie doubted it had ever been opened and after a few moments of barging his shoulder against the thing he gave up, massaging the pain that had set up shop in his arm as a result of his exertions. No doubt there would be a massive bruise there come the morning.

There was nothing else for it, he would have to climb over. Reggie looked about for something, anything, that he could use to get a boost up over the fence. In the blackness of the alley it was very hard to see much of anything and in the end he was forced to traipse all the way back the way that he had come in order to drag the filthy mattress that had waylaid him earlier back to the old man's yard so that he could use that to give him the extra height he needed. In the end Reggie had to contrive to somehow fold the mattress in half just so that it would give him enough of a leg up.

Now that he was standing on top of the folded mattress he could peer over inside Old Mister Andersen's yard. There was just one window overlooking the yard, but fortunately for Reggie the light was off and the curtains were drawn. There was no danger of him being spotted.

Of the geese there was no visible sign and they were no longer making any noise at this point (presumably they had gone to sleep), however, he could see a little wooden hut with a ramp outside leading up to an opening just large enough for geese to enter. Or a man the size of Mr Andersen to crawl in on hands and knees. Reggie hoped that it would be big enough to admit him as well.

There was only one way to find out. Reggie grabbed a hold of the top of the fence and began to pull himself up over it. Somehow in the process of pulling himself across the threshold he managed to be dangling head first over the other side of the fence with his feet waving helplessly in the air. Reggie really wanted to cry out for help as he felt himself slipping, but he dared not in case the old man heard him. He ended up falling like a sack of potatoes and landing in an undignified heap in a pile of compost.

Reggie stood up groggily with bruises on top of his bruises and smelling like an outhouse that hadn't been cleaned for a week. He hoped that all of this was worth it. With as much dignity as he could muster Reggie straightened his now dented trilby upon his mussed-up hair and crept towards the hut. At the ramp he got down on his hands and knees, he was already dirty so what did a little goose shit matter, and he clambered up into the domain of the geese.

It was dark inside so he could barely see a thing. With one hand he reached into his jacket pocket and pulled out his phone, switching on its inbuilt torch.

Arranged around where he now knelt was a collection of six nests, each with another smaller ramp leading up to it. Each nest was occupied by a goose. What kind of goose Reggie did not know, to his untrained eyes they looked just like your average everyday goose with white feathers and a yellow beak. Running under each nest there were six tubes that connected to a larger tube that fed out into a newspaper lined basket that lay on the floor in the centre of the hut.

Inside the basket there were several eggs. Some were normal white, speckled goose eggs and some were golden... just like the ones that Old Mister Andersen had been bringing to Reggie's pawn brokers for the last few months. There was no way of knowing, however, which goose the golden eggs had come from.

"Very clever," Reggie muttered dryly.

Old Mister Andersen had somehow acquired himself a goose that laid golden eggs straight out of a fairy tale, but he'd also gotten himself five decoys so that stealing it would be nearly impossible.

Reggie sat down in a cross-legged position on the floor in front of the assembled nests and began to think. How was he going to do this? One way or another he was going to leave with that goose.

Perhaps there was some sort of distinguishing mark on the golden egg laying goose that set it apart from the others?

Reggie stood up as high as the low roof of the hut would allow and peered closely at each slumbering bird in turn. As far as he could tell they were all identical.

How could the old man guarantee that each goose would sit exactly over the hole in the bottom of their nest? Maybe not every egg made it into the basket at the bottom.

Maybe there could be a tell-tale golden egg sitting under the correct goose right at this very moment.

Reggie moved closer to the nearest goose, laying his phone down beside it so that the light would help him see into the nest, and thrust his hands under the sleeping bird, lifting it bodily off its nest. Christ, it was heavy! Please let this be the right one, he prayed silently. He looked down into the nest. The padded walls of the roosting spot were inclined in such a fashion as to allow any eggs to roll right down into the hole provided, even if the bird wasn't sitting exactly over it.

"Shit!" Reggie hissed.

He looked up under the goose's bottom on the off chance that there would be a golden egg protruding from whatever orifice it produced them from. Nothing.

And then he noticed the goose was looking down on him, wide awake with red eyes.

It hissed and opened its beak. Reggie couldn't help but notice that the edges were extremely serrated.

The goose flapped its wings, and though they had been clipped to prevent it from ever flying off they were sufficient to enable the bird to land on its webbed feet without serious injury.

Reggie snatched up his phone and backed away from the angry goose, hitting his head on the low ceiling as he did so and he realised that he'd have to turn his back on the thing and crawl out on his hands and knees if he was to get away.

The goose honked and hissed loudly, flapping its wings menacingly as it advanced on the hapless pawn broker. And then the inevitable happened.

The other geese woke up too.

Upon seeing Reggie the five geese hissed in unison and raised their feathery bottoms off of their nests. As the third one got up, Reggie could swear that he saw a golden egg pop out of its rear and tumble into the hole beneath.

Though his mind was screaming at him to get out of there, upon seeing the goose with the golden egg, Reggie's first instinct was to make a grab for it. He lunged for the goose with both hands and managed to wrap his fingers around its neck.

And then the other geese attacked.

They leapt off their nests in a furious flurry of flapping wings and flying feathers and threw themselves at the intruder, pecking and biting and stabbing with their pointed beaks.

Reggie yelped in pain as blood burst forth from the dozens of lacerations caused by the fowl assault and he let go of the golden egg laying goose. Once free, the magic bird joined its fellows in attacking Reggie, and the pawn broker soon lost sight of which bird he was after in the ensuing melee of beaks and feathers. Reggie found himself forced to his knees by the sheer weight of the attacking birds and he tried to crawl out of the hut to get away from them. As he went, the six geese were with him every step of the way pecking and biting and beating him with their wings. His clothes were torn, his skin cut and bleeding in more places than he could now count. Some of the cuts were deep and he could feel himself getting dizzy from blood loss.

Reggie somehow made it down the ramp, rolling part of the way, and he started to crawl towards the fence. And then one beak stabbed into his left eyeball and tore it free from the socket.

Reggie screamed in agony, his hand reaching instinctively for the ruined mess where his eye had once been and he tumbled forward to land face first in the compost heap that had broken his fall earlier. The geese fell upon his prone body and continued to tear strips of flesh from him as he lay there. As Reggie felt himself being slowly suffocated by the compost, too weak to get up, a dim part of his brain realised that they were eating him alive.

Old Mister Andersen had come outside five minutes ago to investigate the commotion. He stood there watching as his pets devoured Reggie's pathetic remains.

"Dearie me," the old man muttered sadly. "It looks like I'm going to have to find another pawn broker. At this rate there won't be any left in town. Will I ever find an honest man who's worth his weight in golden eggs?"

12days Of Christmas:2017

5. Gold Rings
Em Dehaney

I

Francine was my first wife. She was young and I was impatient. I harried that girl day and night to marry me. Every time I saw her at the corner store, buying groceries for her folks, I'd shout, 'When you gon' marry me, Miss Francine?'

She would just look down at the ground. But I could see her blushing, even through all them freckles. I turned up at the house one night, stood on that front porch with June-bugs flying all around, and I called for her Pa. I asked for her hand in marriage, all proper like. He had eight mouths to feed, not including him and his cold-fish of a wife, so one less under his roof would be a blessing. He didn't even ask Francine if she wanted to.

We married in the spring, full of innocence. Francine at least. I knew what I was doin'. The first time I shoved myself inside her she was dry and scared, and she tried buck me off like a mad little March mule. It never changed. I liked it that way. Her hair was so thin, it used to come away in my hands. I'll never forget the colour. Pale and clean as fresh bedsheets, and how it looked stained with blood like those same sheets on our wedding night.

I never meant for it to happen that way. It was all accidental. The baby. The fall down the stairs that left us childless and her barren at eighteen. Such a clumsy girl, that one. Even her Pa used to say it. Always walking into somethin' or droppin' the goddamn groceries. When I saw her lying there, all bent and crooked, a bloody mess, screaming and crying, I got as hard as ever had in my whole rotten life.

She was never the same after that. She didn't fight no more, just lay there, like a doll.

It was a sad day when she fell in front of that freight train.

2

Paulette was my second wife. I met her at the market, the handsome young widow. Everyone knew the story of my pale and crazy bride who took a leap in front of a train, stricken with grief. All the ladies in town got the soft eyes whenever I was around. There he goes, poor thing. I could look after him real good.

Boy, could that woman cook. I ate like a king when she was around. Coca-cola hams. Creamy mash potatoes and gravy. Peach cobbler. Buttermilk pancakes and candied bacon. I was fixin' to get fat as a stuck pig. My gut got so large I could barely see over it. She was a sturdy girl too. How her ass used to wobble when she ran away from me, how I could grab handfuls of overfilled sausage flesh when I finally caught up. I liked to bite into her, feel my teeth sliding through that buttery behind. She was meaty and creamy, like a fine steak.

I sure miss that Paulette. Shame she had such a smart mouth. Always running, like our old diesel genny. That genny needed a few good whacks with a wrench every now and again too, to keep it quiet.

Paulette don't run her mouth so much now it's fulla dirt and she's buried in the apple yard.

3

Lillie-May was my third wife. Met her at the roadhouse out on Breakneck Hill. She was a hellcat, that one. Thought she liked it rough. She had no idea. Daddy issues, that what they call it? Her Daddy was on his way to becoming a State Senator, had the money and the right connections. The only thing that stood in his way was that druggy dive-bar slut of a daughter. A career in politics means no skeletons in the closet. Or buried under the porch. Or wrapped in a blanket and rolled over a ravine.

Lillie-May loved to make her Daddy angry, to make him fret, and most of all, make him jealous. I saw the way his eyes lingered over her thighs when she wore them little shorts of hers. I could read his mind, picturing himself sliding a finger up inside them shorts, slipping it between her lips, then taking it out and getting a real good sniff of his daughter's delicious juices. And you what? I think she saw it too. And I think she liked it.

They found her hog-tied and branded, dumped by the side of the road after I skipped town. I never broke her neck, but that pretty little skull of hers was sure smashed in after I'd finished with it. I think I did her Daddy a favour, won him the sympathy votes.

4

Jackie was my fourth wife. Jackie, Jackie, O Jackie. Told her my name was Jack. Jack and Jackie, what a couple. Just like the Kennedys. I was new in town and she had a friendly face. She was one of them mousey types, you know the ones. Hair the colour they was born with, never wear a skirt over the knee, like helpin' the homeless and pretendin' they don't suck a dick. She said she had never met anyone like me before, I told her the same. I wasn't lying. I had never met a thirty year old woman who hadn't gotten drunk. I had never met a thirty year old woman who still had stuffed animals on her bed. I had never met a thirty year old woman who was savin' herself for the right man. I fixed all that in one goddamned night. Proposed to her over a cheap Mexican dinner and told her the cocktails were virgin, just like her. Took her tipsy ass home, dumped her on the bed and played stuff the animals 'til morning. She threw 'em all out soon after. Reckoned they smelled funny.

She used to talk about startin' a family, all her friends were expecting. Her friends thought I was cute. She did too, 'til I ripped her wedding dress. Fixin' to pack her things and go back to her mother that very night, she was. I took the lace veil from her hair, tied it round her neck and twisted 'til her eyes popped. O Jackie, you weren't expecting that.

5

Jack was my first husband. I knew that wasn't his name, just like mine wasn't Sally. Everyone has their secrets. We played house for a while, as the thunder clouds rolled. Oh, he had a cruel way and a dark eye, but he was handsome as The Devil. He said I was his one and only, and I believed him 'til the day I found four gold bands hidden in a beat up old tobaccy tin in his top drawer. One of the rings had a wisp of hair tied round it. The blood stain had long since turned from red to brown, but I knew it was blood all the same. I put those rings back where I found 'em and made believe like they weren't there. 'Til the first time he whipped me so hard with his belt that my back split in two. Then all I could think about was those four gold rings, and how I was as sure as goddamn not gonna be number five.

I was a good girl. I waited and watched. I listened and learned. Sure, I got a few bruises, but it was worth it. The time had to be right.

Jack was my only husband. I took a straight razor to his throat while he slept off a rotgut hangover, slicing through turkey-neck and vocal chords. And when he opened his eyes in shock, putting his hands up to stem the gushing blood, I took that razor downtown and cut off the only thing he ever really loved. His gurgles and spurts filled the air like wedding bells as I threaded five gold rings on his limp and bloodied dick, and threw it out the window.

'Til death do you part.

4. Calling Birds
Anthony Cowin

Bad Mouth spreads like a shadow through city streets, a menacing sunset stealing the light from innocent lives. It burgles houses where troubled minds sleep. It creeps up stairwells, slips under bedroom doors and crawls into the throat resting, ready for the morning. Sheltered under flickering red candles.

The next evening it floats through twinkling lights. A wall of mist is no rival for Bad Mouth. It holds and focuses on her body in the bathtub.

It falls. Bad Mouth is a camera. It records everything. Keeps the snapshots alive in a dark memory. A flipbook of horrors thumbed into action, ready to show the world.

China Cole lays under foam and flowers. Her unfurled hand droops over the porcelain like a dead rosebud, dripping blood onto the snow-white bathmat. Red that meanders through the grout creating a maze, haemorrhaging gates that enclose her grief. The razor embedded in her palm severed her lifeline. The foetus hangs beneath the film of petals and soap scum. She'd sliced it from her belly. It's tangled in her entrails like a baby mermaid caught in fresh elodea. The cause of the gossip ripped and pulled from inside her. A caesarean of loose talk. The child grew with each rumour, fattened with every whispered insult. The words choked in her throat, snaked through her brain, and bled through her ears.

China hid in the stalls at her work Christmas party, feet tucked into the small round of her belly. The drunken whispers reflected off the mirrors outside, smeared among the red lipstick onto mouths that spat dark words. With each tale, her baby grew.

She reached out for solace in the quiet of prayers. A murmur of nuns gawked at her, passing notes during communion. The baby doubled in size during Christmas hymns. The end of mass brought echoes in place of harmonies. She cradled beneath the pews in agony. Every black whisper makes the bad secrets grow. Until eventually they end up like China Cole's baby floating in piss and petals. And red on the bathmat.

Bad Mouth claims another victim. Or two.

***

Three towns over and a lifetime away a child sits crying in a schoolyard. A wooden skipping rope handle knocks her with a decaying regularity as the roundabout it's tied to slows behind her. A teacher looks up from the register at the empty chair in his classroom. Through a meteor shower of condensation on the window, he sees her outside in the yard as the roundabout stops. He scrapes his chair back with such force the kids know it's a surrogate for yelling. They wait for him to leave before scampering from their desks to gather at the window. Peeking out through scissored snowflakes clinging to the glass.

The child in the yard considers the rope. Thinks of untying it and using it for a different purpose. She hears the words in her mind again. The bad words about her father. She punches two fists against her ears as though the sounds are real, solid, alive and she can deafen herself from their taunting. Eventually her knuckles are red from striking the bone of her skull.

"He's a monster." Another punch.

"He's a wolf." Another hit.

"*He's the Bad Man.*" A whisper close to her ear.

Bad Mouth teases the words through the trickling blood from her ears. A thesaurus of hate twisted inside her DNA.

The teacher is standing above her as the sound grows in her mind. The bad words echo through the labyrinth of her consciousness. The teacher is talking but she can't hear him. He begins shouting; yelling at her, spit flying from his dry lips, clinging to his dirty blonde moustache. She's never seen him angry.

He grabs her wrists so hard the right one sprains instantly.

Later, after the child's mother watched him disappear from the small rectangular window at back of the ambulance the teacher finally spoke to himself.

"I'm the *Bad Man*."

The Headmistress pulled him to her chest, assuring him he's not bad, it's not his fault.

She doesn't understand. The words were not about him. They were a confession sharpened into arrows that struck from the child's mind.

The girl was called Sophie and her dad lived in a place called prison. She lived in a two-bedroom council flat with her mum and younger sister. Sophie was eleven and Georgia was six. She never knew her mother's age, but she often heard people whisper that she looked old for it. Sophie listened to her mother's pleas and kept the family secrets hidden. That's what families do she was told.

"It'll make you special Soph. It'll make you strong," her mother had lied.

Of course, it did nothing of the sort. She realised that the first night he crept past her bed and headed toward Georgia.

Sophie had felt guilty about the relief that kept her biting her tongue that night. But like the bad words, the guilt also grew. She told a teacher who whispered into a phone. His eyes looking at her in rhythm as though she was a beat too risky to dance with.

Her mother collected her from school with eyes full of swords.

The school dealt with everything, followed their protocol, so no child would know. But of course, parents spoke when the newspapers reported the case. At first even they didn't take much interest. Sophie began to think she'd dreamt it all, or imagined having a father. Her mother convinced her she had a strange and vivid imagination. Too many times her mum told Sophie those lies as she pushed her from her shoulder. The blades in her eyes glinted toward her husband.

But soon, like the echoes in Sophie's mind, the words in the tabloids grew bigger. Twelve-point footnotes became block headlines. Skinny to bold. Berliner to Helvetica. Whispers to screams. Then the headlines leaked onto the pavements and rolled along the gutters. The bad words gathered in pools like black rain, melted ink that stuck to the soles of the children's shoes as they walked through the school gates. By the time the home bell rang the footprints stained the whole school. The caretaker buffed the tiles, but nothing cleaned away those tar stains. The words gathered together. They gain strength from huddling.

They whispered at first. As though they were not sure how to be words any more. But soon they began screaming.

The ambulance turned into the hospital.

The back doors swung open.

The fluorescent strip lights above the trolley reminded Sophie of comet tails and she wanted to be back in class. Making Christmas cards for parents she hated. She closed her eyes away from the silent world. Inside her head the bad words roared in tamed echoes like circus lions.

Lights burnt through her eyelids painting red lines above her eyes like two bowls of bright spaghetti. The doctor smiled at her as she opened them. He looked around the room as though checking they were alone.

"Bitchwitch. Witchbitch. Whore," he screamed at her suddenly and so close she could smell the fried onions on his breath.

She blinked and saw him outside behind the glass, grinning in the corridor deep in thought at the papers in his hand. She tried not close her eyes again, but tiredness had other intentions.

Bad Mouth investigated the hospital; a camera looking for a scoop. It slid easily under private doors and into open wards. No need for a gurney. It snaked up through masks strapped to old people's mouths, filling them with bile. Nurses looked at each other differently; a doctor lingering a moment too long at a nurse station was now an adulterer. The surgeon blinking too often through the letterbox eyes of his mask was fantasising about anaesthesiologists. Bad Mouth moaned and exhaled. Bad Mouth recorded and changed the script. Black words smudge across the white walls of the hospital. No longer sterile. Graffiti of guilt.

Sophie dreamt of roundabouts and skipping ropes. It was a bright day, the sky lit by two hanging fluorescent tubes in place of a sun. The children sang nursery rhymes in mechanical beeps like the medical apparatus in the private room. Sophie took in a deep breath and smiled. The school kitchen offered aromas of roast potatoes and fried chicken. Her favourite. Another deep breath searching for gravy and steamed veg found only sterilising fluids and hand soap. The roundabout rolled toward her, spinning faster as it lifted off the ground. The skipping rope, tied to it swooped like nunchaku. She ducked, too late, her head hit the underneath of the metal disc.

She woke in the hospital. It did smell of chicken and potatoes. An aching hunger smashed against her. Her mum sat in the corner, her sister read comics in an adjacent room visible through panelled windows latticed with wire.

Her mother looked up. She was speaking to her, but no words came out. She could tell her mum had been crying but she felt no pity for her. As Sophie's mum came closer to the bed she could make out a thin voice. She was clutching a handkerchief to her mouth as though trying to stuff the words back down her own throat. She sat on the chair next to the bed, took her daughter's hand and twisted the sprained wrist. She screamed at Sophie in metallic anger.

"Bitch. Witch. Whore." Her voice flatlined.

Sophie closed her eyes as the bad words grew. She wanted to die, push away the pain from her wrist and her ears, but mostly from her mind.

Bad Mouth gurgled in a drip connected to her skin. It stabbed into her veins through the broken flesh. It felt at home in there.

Her mother walked the corridors looking for a machine that pissed out weak coffee. She could really do with a drink she thought; something strong would be nice. As she idly dreamt about buying a bottle of vodka, an overweight cleaner leant on her mop pole and stared at her.

After a while the cleaner walked over to the vending machine.

"Terrible coffee in here. More caffeine in rain water I bet." Sophie's mum nodded without turning to face her.

"We all need a little something to pick us up hey?" The cleaner left the mop balanced in the bucket and leant forward. "You helped *him*," she whispered into her ear.

"No. I never did," she said, unable to turn. The woman pressed against her head. Her skin stank of disinfectant and day-old cigarettes.

"If he's the bad man then you're the bad woman. You should be locked up too."

The plastic cup dropped to the floor as the pain caused an earthquake in her head. The cleaner pulled away and smiled.

"Guess I got me some cleaning to do."

Sophie's mum pushed her palms to her temples wishing she had that vodka right then. She ran from the corridor, knocking the cleaning woman's shoulder, and sped out into the street. She passed the ambulance bay, ran through the gates, and didn't stop until she found a store, ignoring the

Santa with a rattling donation tin in the doorway. Inside she bought a bottle of Russian Standard and took it back to the hospital. She found an unlocked private bathroom and emptied the bottle into her stomach in thirty minutes. Every swig tasted like oily words. Every drop nicked her throat like razor wire. All the time the cleaner's accusations echoed in her mind.

Before she finished the bottle, she could hear every whisper in the hospital. Frail old women used their dying words to taunt her from their beds. Visitors clutching grapes in brown paper bags made bitter wine spill from their accusatory mouths. Surgeons sliced up their words with scalpels of hate. Each one of them screamed their whispers directly into her brain. The cleaner found her corpse in the closet when she finished her night shift the following morning. Bad Mouth had come outside visiting hours.

Bad Mouth gurgled in her bloated liver. The invisible killer who spoke too much.

The four nuns at the funeral huddled together like magpies waiting to steal gold from the dead. Sophie didn't care. She'd lost her little sister to a foster home and her own life was a map undrawn. The solicitor had said there was little money, her mother's death was considered suicide by the insurance company so that was a lost cause. One of the younger nuns cupped her hand to whisper into the ear of an elderly magpie. One for sorrow. The old bird looked across the open grave at Sophie and grinned. She knew Bad Mouth had come to pay his last respects, maybe pick up a few new clients while he was there. Funerals are a great place to network and Bad Mouth never let a secret be untold.

Sophie cupped her own hand as she scooped up dark earth. A worm wriggled inside the soil, poking out as she threw the muck onto her mother's coffin. There were no flowers or family. No petals or warmth.

The priest coughed awkwardly, making the nuns stop their school girl whispering and bow to the wounded ground.

"Eternal rest give to them, O Lord," he bellowed. "And let perpetual light shine upon them. Shine so bright their dark and bitchy deeds can no longer be hidden."

Sophie looked up at the priest who was smiling as he recited the liturgy. She looked across to the nuns who were all whispering, giggling and pointing fingers at the child. Four birds the colour of coal and dirty snow.

The priest continued, "May God forgive them for being whores. May they rot in Hell." He slammed the Bible shut and walked away, the nuns following like ducks in a row now, no longer preying magpies.

Sophie stood at the graveside alone and waited for her counsellor to arrive. All the time the whispers and words floated across the cemetery, rustled through the browning leaves on the trees and screamed at her. Words scraped away the soil from the top of her mother's coffin, worms reached out like fingers of accusation, clawing through the soil to point up at her.

The sky blackened with the dark words. Bad Mouth chiselled insults and rumours on gravestones. Sophie closed her eyes and fell into the open ground. When she awoke she was in the councillor's car speeding toward the hospital. She never thought of her mother and father again for the rest of her life until her little sister's funeral.

Georgia had been adopted by the foster family on her seventh birthday. Sophie had lost all contact with her, though she tried and failed to find her on several occasions. Sophie's life had been uneventful. She worked a boring job in a shop selling garments to boring ladies. She eventually became manager of the store and realised on her thirtieth birthday she'd be in that job until she retired. There'd been one or two men in her life, but nothing ever lasted. She couldn't bear to be touched.

However, Sophie had gone on several dates recently with a salesman who dropped by with samples every fortnight. He was kind and charming, like a favourite uncle, one of the shop girls had commented. Sophie figured he must be fifteen years older than her and ready to settle down. To her surprise, she found herself falling in love. The night he proposed they went to a hotel in town for a meal. He booked a room and paid the concierge to send up a bottle of champagne.

Sophie tried to make love to him, she really wanted to. Even if it was just to make him happy. But it didn't work. The words came back, the whispers hissing in the fizzing wine in her glass. Lies bursting free from escaping bubbles. She saw a man on top of her she didn't recognise. A man that smelt like chicken and roast potatoes. A man that reminded her of fluorescent rods and screeching magpies as he heaved away. She couldn't understand why the images kept flashing in her head. He wrapped a skipping rope around her neck and grinned. She snapped up. No rope, no bad man.

Her fiancé climbed off, pointing and fumbling as he raced to the bathroom. When he returned she was still confused. He rolled up two white towels and placed them against her head on either side. They soaked with the blood from her ears within a minute. Blooms of red on virgin white pillows.

Frank said he understood when she handed back the ring the following day. Though she knew he never really did. Magpies never give back gold and diamonds she'd thought as she walked out of the hotel. Sophie decided men and love were just two things that were never going to be part of her life. She continued working at the store and eating alone every night.

One morning she was called from the shop floor into the office by her assistant. As the young girl handed her the phone, Sophie noticed her hand was shaking. The assistant moved past her boss, but remained at the door, leaning against the jamb.

"Hi. Yes this is she." She shrugged her shoulders at her assistant only to be met with a slight shake of her bowing head.

"I'm sorry no, you must have the wrong person. Yes, that's my name but I don't know anybody called that."

After a few moments of nodding Sophie placed the receiver down and returned to the store front. Her assistant followed her, knowing what the call was about and confused by the reaction of her boss.

"I remember him now," Sophie said as she slumped on a chair by the window display.

"Your father you mean?" her assistant asked.

"Yes, and well, no. Not him. I know that's how they found me, but it's the other one," she said

"Which other one?"

"Bad Mouth," Sophie said standing up. She straightened her skirt and walked from the shop. She left her apartment door open as she packed an overnight bag. She didn't want to wait around in case *He* came to visit. She told her assistant she'd only be two days, three at most, from the payphone at the railway station over the crackling tannoy announcements.

Sophie travelled to a hospital where she was greeted by a dour looking man who told him to follow her. She walked along a red line that travelled through the corridors, turning at right angles and dipping down slopes through a curtain of split plastic sheets.

She looked at the body on the slab and nodded. She leant over and took the cold hand and kissed it.

"So, you confirm the identity?" the mortician asked.

"Yes," Sophie said. "Only the name is different. It says China Cole on her tag."

"She was adopted we understand," the mortician said. He looked up into Sophie's eyes. "Both parents died when she was young but not before they'd changed her name and moved out here. The nuns took her in after that. Raised her till she was eighteen."

Sophie nodded with each word though not really taking it all in.

"Can I ask you a question?" the mortician said pulling back the white sheet over the body.

"Of course," Sophie said looking down, trying to catch one more look at the beautiful dead woman before she was covered.

"What was her name when you knew her?"

"Georgia," she said finally allowing herself to weep. "Her name was Georgia and she was my little sister."

Sophie remembered her father and her mother as she buried her sister and her unborn child. The child she'd cut out of herself in a bath of roses. She remembered the terror of bedtime, the wetting herself in school, the teasing and the words.

She went back to her hotel after the funeral. No need for a wake with only her and the priest present. She specifically demanded that no nuns attend. Those black birds always brought Bad Mouth along as an uninvited guest. An empty-handed gate crasher who stole from the party.

She took a bottle of vodka from a brown paper bag and poured herself a large drink. After two or three more, she lay on her bed and thought of nothing until she drifted off to sleep.

In the morning she packed her bag and headed home, telling herself to pop into the store first before going to her apartment. She held the photograph of China Cole in her hands on the train and remembered her sister Georgia. She felt guilt and shame and a terrible weight of loss.

Two nuns whispered to each other a few seats down on the other side of the aisle. Sophie looked at them and smiled. They smiled back and giggled like schoolgirls, the younger one pointing to a handsome man in the seat opposite. Two older nuns tutted at them making their faces turn sour.

Maybe Bad Mouth still lurks in the shadows of Sophie's life. But for that moment at least he was gone. He was invisible and silent. Sophie fell asleep and thought of chicken and roast potatoes. She promised herself it would be the first meal she'd have when she got home. Maybe she'd invite Frank around to join her. Maybe things would be different with her now. Now locks had fallen open in her life, piling to rust at her feet.

Frank stepped into the store and greeted Sophie's assistant. They shared a pot of tea and a small saucer of biscuits. It was cloudy outside, the sky darkening by the minute, threatening snow and maybe a thunderstorm. When Frank stepped back into the street, the snow fell as though commanded by the tingle of the bell above the shop door. He'd left a case of samples for Sophie to look at when she arrived back, all bright colours and fresh patterns. He'd also left a dark item, an item so black it seemed to bring the storm clouds inside the shop. It wasn't for sale. This one was free for all to sample

Sophie's assistant stared at the crumbs on the saucer and grinned. Frank had shared something so delicate it made her feel vibrant and giddy. She picked up the telephone and rang head office. She made three more calls before Sophie arrived back at the shop. Before she'd killed the ring of the bell with the shop door, she felt it. Sophie recognised the black garment that hung there among the shedding tinsel and pine air freshener. The shroud that had always hung over her life.

The words grew inside her, inseminated her and threatened to be born before she could sit. Outside, a storm of headlines whispered in the winds. Black rain wet the pavements with oil and ink. White snow turning to grey sludge. It fell from umbrellas that made a roof of the city. Every passer-by turned their head toward Sophie inside the store. Bad Mouth would never give up. Not while people fed it. Not while people remained hungry themselves.

Four nuns stood at the shop window, grinning. Four birds as black as coal and dirty snow. Sophie felt a kick inside her stomach. The nuns laughed and strolled off into the lightning like colly birds caught in a staggered strobe effect. Sophie's belly began to swell and burn.

Bad Mouth has a new victim.

12days Of Christmas:2017

3. French Hens
Peter Germany

The shed looked good, for a cheapy from the catalogue. Jeff was pleased with it and thought it fit in nicely. The enclosure took up half the garden, but it would give the hens a decent stretch of grass to run around and shit on.

With the coup now built he went to their garden shed, not the one that was now a chicken house, and carried out the bags of sawdust and straw. He put a liberal layer down on the floor of the run, which he'd already laid lino on. Then a few handfuls of straw went down. He didn't know why they needed both straw and sawdust but Leah had been adamant they did. With that done he filled up the feed tray and pulled the hose pipe out to fill the twenty-five litre water hopper. He added a guesstimate of Red Mite solution and a tonic he was pretty sure was just overpriced vinegar and waited for the water to fill the hopper. Time ceased to advance while he waited. Jeff was pretty sure somewhere in the infinite universe a species evolved into intelligence, and then annihilated itself in the time it took to fill the water container for the three chickens Leah was buying.

The water spilled over the top as Jeff was wondering if he could teach chickens to play football. "Oh for fucks sake." He pulled the hose out and screwed the lid on.

"We're home!" Leah proclaimed as she came through the side gate with their cat carrier in one hand.

"Tell me you only bought the three we agreed?" He was comforted by the lack of additional transport cases, but that didn't mean there wasn't more in her car.

"Of course, you phoning the man up telling him not to sell us any more than three this time round displays a lack of faith in my self-control."

"We've got four cats, we'd said we have two. Rex is still traumatised by that." The Labrador barked his agreement.

"Rex loves the kitties, so do you. And we couldn't let them go into a cattery."

"Your dopey sister should never have got them in the first place. She can barely look after herself."

"Exactly, we had to take them in."

"One morning I swear I'm going to wake up to find a bean stalk growing out of the garden."

"That won't happen, I don't like beans."

"No but I bet you'd like a golden goose."

"Ooo, we could get geese."

"Stop right there, no geese. We've barely got room for the chickens. Rex has already lost half his garden." Rex barked again.

"Meanie."

"Yep, but you love me anyway."

Leah gave him a smile full of childlike excitement as she stepped into the run. "It looks good. I'm glad we built our own one. For what those coups cost online this was money well spent."

She placed the carrier on the ground and opened the front. Nothing came out. She frowned. "Come on girls, it's all safe out here. Look, food."

"Give them a chance, so far today they've been chased around their home, pushed into a carrier that probably still stinks of cat piss from when we took Eisenhower to be neutered last month. They've had to put up with your driving, and now they're in an environment that they don't yet know. So unless you're gonna drag them out or turn the carrier on its end and tip them out, leave them to come out when they're ready."

"Don't crap on my driving, I've not got a speeding ticket in two months," Leah said as she stepped out of the chicken run.

"No, but you did run over a traffic warden."

"That's an exaggeration, I only nudged her."

"After you forgot to change gear from first to reverse. It's a good thing she had a sense of humour."

"It's in the wrong place on that car,"

"Come on, let's have a cup of tea."

Leah jumped up from the kitchen table just as Jeff was pouring the milk into their cups.

"Look, they're out. Yay!"

"How long till they start laying?"

"The man said they were already laying, but we probably won't get any for a couple of days due to the stress of the move. We need to start thinking about names."

"I've got names for them."

"Jeff, we're not calling them Vindaloo, Korma, or Tikka."

"And you say I'm no fun." He looked out to the hens. "How are you going to tell them apart? They're all the same colour."

"We'll figure that out later. We could get them jumpers!"

"How'd that work out with the cats?"

Leah scrunched her nose up as she looked at their two older cats, who were laying in the kitchen window sunbathing. "You may have a point there."

"Refresh my memory," Jeff said as the hens quickly began to eat, "How did you persuade me that chickens were a good idea?"

"Remember last month, when you wanted the cash for Bristol Horror?"

Jeff nodded.

"Well you said I could have anything if we could find the cash for the convention; thus, chickens!" That excited grin again. He was glad he'd managed to find someone who could still get this excited by life.

"I'm pretty sure I've been screwed here, you like the cons as much as I do."

She grinned.

Jeff finished, put the teas on the table and watched as the chickens explored their new home. They were Leah's project, but he liked animals. His dream was to have a house with a chunk of land and have a few dozen chickens, geese, ducks, goats, and maybe a few pigs as well. They were a good twenty years away from that, but with how hard they both worked and how good Leah was with money, it would happen one day.

"How about Alice, Lemmy, and Ozzy?"

"Yes, that's perfect!" Leah said. "Come on, let's go and see them."

Jeff, mug of tea in hand, followed his excited girlfriend out to the chicken run. Their big brave dog, Rex, watched the new arrivals from the other side of the garden. The younger cats, Monty and Eisenhower were both stalking the hens while the older two, Tom and Jerry, were still sunbathing in the kitchen window.

"They're so cute."

Jeff dropped to his haunches, the grass was too damp to sit on, and took in the three young hens. He had to admit they were very pretty, with a deep and rich reddish brown plumage.

"What type of hens are they?"

Leah shrugged. "I don't know. I liked their colouring."

"I'll have a look in one of the books later."

One of the hens suddenly charged at the netting, Monty fled in the other direction. "We need to set up some cameras for this shit."

It took Rex four days to get the guts to go up to the chicken run, and when he did he got pecked on the nose. That, Jeff did manage to get on video. Tom and Jerry were still not showing much interest in the hens. Monty and Eisenhower were, but to no avail; the hens didn't seem fazed by anything. Jeff suspected they knew they couldn't be got at behind the netting. He'd quickly realised they weren't stupid animals. They knew what the bag of corn looked like, they knew what sound the shed door made when opened. As well as the back door and the side gate. Any movement in the garden or house resulted in an ordinance of the hens. They were nosey buggers to say the least. Noisy as well. If they weren't let out the moment the sun began to rise they weren't afraid to voice their displeasure. They also didn't like it when you went into the henhouse when they were in there. Leah had stuck to her promise of looking after the hens, but she'd been caught in traffic and had asked him to collect the eggs and lock them up for the night.

The coup was in the enclosure and he made sure to shut the gate when he'd gone in, leaving a jealous Rex wagging his tail outside. Jeff shut down the metal hatch that the hens used to go in and out and then went to the side of the coup and opened the full sized door. Immediately the three hens started clucking off at this disturbance.

"Oh shut up," Jeff said. He noticed they were laying in the two nesting boxes he'd rigged up. They were simply plastic washing bowls resting in a wooden frame he'd made. The hens were totally ignoring the perches he'd built for them.

He picked each of the three grumpy chickens up and put them on the perch, each one mouthing off more so as he did.

"I come to steal your unborn children from you and you are powerless to prevent me from doing such! Mwahahahaha."

He got the two eggs and backed out of the coup, making sure the hens didn't make a dash for freedom. Eggs in hand he went out of the enclosure, to find a happy Rex and juggled the eggs as he walked back to the house thinking about scrambled eggs for breakfast.

The following week, Jeff looked into the coup and was glad he had a box of nitrile gloves he'd got from the guy who supplied his work. Leah was in the house, suffering from one of the worst head colds he'd known her have. The fact that she was in bed was testament to just how ill she was.

He looked again at the coup, it hadn't been cleaned out last week as they did it every other week. He kind of wished he hadn't suggested that.

"Ah well, it's only shit." He dropped down to his hands and knees and went into the henhouse and started to pull the sawdust to him. Jeff ignored the feeling of chicken shite squishing between his fingers.

One of the hens came into the house and hopped onto a perch, the first time he'd noticed one of them using it.

"Alright sweetheart, you gonna give me a hand?" The chicken twitched its head but didn't give any other reply.

It stayed there as Jeff began to scoop the dirty litter into a flexi tub. It was full to the brim and he thought he'd be able to get another handful in it so went down for more, but felt something flicking against his back and neck. Behind him one of the other two chickens stood atop the stacked soiled litter, flicking the stuff at him with her feet.

"Really?" The chicken gave a cluck and flicked more sawdust at him. "Fuck off."

Again, a cluck and more flicking. The hen jumped off as he reached to pick it up and ran to the far end of the enclosure where Rex was sitting and fronted up to the dog. He was out of range so he wasn't bothered.

After taking the tub to the compost heap, he returned and began to fill it up again. The hen that sat herself on the perch was still there, and didn't move as he went under the perch to get to the last of the dirty litter. He felt something land on his ear and run down the side of his neck, it made him tense his shoulders up and he moved back and sat upright. Jeff felt behind his ear and his hand came back with a smear of fresh, runny shit.

"I'm not afraid to ring your fucking neck," Jeff pointed a finger at the hen, who clucked and hopped, out into the run. "You'd make a great vindaloo!"

With a sigh he finished clearing out the dirty litter, spread some mite powder into the corners of the coup and began to fill it back up with sawdust and straw. As soon as he was done two of the hens rushed in and started raking around in the neatly laid bedding.

As Jeff came out of the coup with half a bag of straw something dropped out of it. He looked down and saw a mouse sprinting for cover. One of the hens grabbed it, and shook it violently. Another of the hens darted out of the house and grabbed the mouse, fighting over it till it was torn apart. Jeff stared in shock as two more mice fell from the bag and tried in vain to flee. The hens grabbed them as well, showing no mercy as they pulled the rodents to pieces and ate them.

Once the last remains of the mice were consumed, the hens went back to their scratching around in the dirt of the run. The vibrant grass was now destroyed by constant pecking from the hens.

Still in shock, Jeff left the run, put the straw and sawdust back in the shed and returned to the house. Out in the garden, the hens kept their eyes him until he was out of sight.

With rain hammering down, Jeff ran out to the chicken run to close the hens up for the night. Leah was out of bed now, but there was no way he was going to let her out in this and have a relapse.

Once he'd slid down the metal hatch he turned and saw Rex sitting in the kitchen doorway looking at him like he was crazy.

Running back to the house he slipped and almost did the splits, and then face planted in the wet grass as he lost control of his body. He rolled onto his back and looked up at the falling rain.

"Fuck it." His words were followed by a chorus from the henhouse. "And you lot can fuck off."

"Are you okay?" Leah called from the kitchen door.

"Yeah, just thought I'd see if the full moon turned me into a werewolf."

"I'm sorry honey," she snuffled through her blocked up nose, "but I don't think that's gonna happen."

"I know, but I can dream. Might show those fucking chickens who's boss."

Jeff woke with a start. Leah slept silently beside him, along with four cats who seemed to have made her their throne. At the foot of the bed Rex snored like a warthog with a cold. If Rex was asleep it can't have been anything to worry about. For all his noise Rex woke at the drop of a pin, or the opening of the fridge.

He could see the sensor light was on outside. He got up and looked down into the garden, but there wasn't anything that shouldn't have been there. The house itself sounded quiet, but he didn't wake up for no reason. He wasn't a light sleeper and he didn't have nightmares. He stood for a moment and listened.

He was feeling uneasy, something had rattled him. Jeff looked at the garden again as the sensor light shut off. It was windy outside, and there was also a couple of million cats that made the garden their playground when the house cats were inside.

He stood there for a few more minutes before getting back into bed, but couldn't settle. After a while he looked at his phone and saw it was almost 5am. He sighed and got up and went downstairs to make a cup of tea. He wasn't going to get asleep again now.

The rise of the sun was hidden by cloud that had rolled in suddenly, bringing rain with it. As the rain was beginning to slowly fall Rex let Jeff know it was time for a run out into the garden to do his boring business. As Rex pelted out the back door Jeff put his wellies on and made his way to the chicken run in just the shorts he slept in. He might as well let them out while he was up, and giving Leah a lay in wasn't a bad idea. She might finally beat that cold in the next day or so.

The chickens were already making a commotion. They made even more noise as he opened the outer door. The three hens ran out. The way they moved always reminded him of dinosaurs in movies.

"You guys haven't forgotten what you evolved from, have you?"

They clucked at him, he smiled and began to turn back to the gate but the three hens lined up in front of him. He backed up slowly as primitive alarm bells went crazy within his body. The gate was just there, but he didn't make it. The hen in the middle launched itself at him, getting a surprising height off the ground. Jeff pushed his arms out to deflect the bird as the other two leapt at him too. He stumbled backwards, hitting his head on the frame of the gate as he fell. The hens took their chance and went for his face. He felt their beaks punching through the flesh of his cheeks. He tried to swat them off, but two the hens went for his eyes. He covered his face and rolled onto his side in the foetal position as the hens pecked and scratched at his bare torso and head.

Rex was barking but the dog couldn't get into the run. Jeff felt a beak grab hold of his earlobe, and then pull. He cried out as the lobe separated from the rest of his ear. He reached out and grabbed one of the hens and threw it across the run, another moved to strike at his now exposed face but he punched it mid-charge. The stunned bird was easy to grab and he snapped its neck and dropped it. The carcass twitched as its sisters resumed their assault with more venom. Jeff got up and launched himself into their attacks, kicking the first one into the side wall of the coup. It hit with a thud and shook its head as the second leapt for his stomach. Jeff caught it, snapped its neck and dropped it. The hen that had bounced off the coup stumped towards him. He stomped on it three times, bones cracking sickeningly with each impact. Something pushed against leg, a chicken with its head hanging to the side was running into his leg. He reached down and picked the bloodied hen up, and tore its head off with a triumphant roar.

Leah trudged sleepily down the stairs, wondering what the hell Rex was barking about and where Jeff was. Rubbing her eyes she walked into the kitchen and gasped. Jeff was standing in the doorway, covered in mud and blood. Rex was stood by his side, a ragged feathery carcass dangling from his mouth.

"About the chickens…"

12days Of Christmas:2017

2. Turtle Doves
Richard Wall

My first guitar saved my life. I wish now that I'd never set eyes on it.

It was 1973.

I was on my way to step out in front of an express train. I knew a place where I could walk onto the track at the very last second, giving the driver no time to brake.

I had it all planned.

When you're an underdeveloped, bespectacled, thirteen-year-old, stammering ginger bookworm, you become the target of choice for every thug, wanker and dickhead looking for a docile recipient for their anger issues.

Dave Scott was Dickhead-in-Chief, with Alex, his twin brother, a very able lieutenant. They were two years older, and their joint mission in life was to seek me out and kick the living shit out of me at every given opportunity. This they did with an amount of pleasure, imagination and attention to detail that was terrifying.

Not that I was a stranger to the dark side of life. I had a brother in the army. Hard as nails he was. But he was killed in Northern Ireland, which caused my dad to drink himself to death, leaving me and my mum on our own. Victims don't attract friends, and with no one to turn to, I lived in my head.

Welcome to my world.

Bullies take your mind to places where rules don't exist. Alone with your thoughts, a maelstrom of anger fuels your imagination. You fantasise about revenge; a hammer to the temple, a knitting needle pushed slowly into the ear, a razor blade dragged across an eyeball, bending a finger back until it snaps with a loud crack. Make them scream, make them bleed, make them beg for mercy. In your mind you're ready for them.

Until the next time. When you turn the corner, and they're waiting, and you piss yourself with fear because you haven't got a hammer, or a knitting needle, or the muscle, expertise or bravery to fight back, and you know damn well that it will be you begging for mercy.

Soon after that your mind tells you that you're worthless, and with no case for the defence you make an appointment for a meeting with the business end of a speeding locomotive.

I was on my way to that meeting when I spotted the guitar propped up next to some dustbins outside the Oxfam shop.

Up until then I had never seen a guitar up close, much less had any desire to play, but when I saw that cheap, wooden acoustic, with nylon strings and plastic tuning pegs, something about it, temporarily distracted me from the dark side of my brain.

There would be another express tomorrow.

I took the guitar home, borrowed a tuition book from the library, and set about devoting every spare minute to practicing. In a very short time I reached the point where I needed something better.

Our neighbour next door-but-one, was a rep for a Mail Order Catalogue. Mum had borrowed a copy and left it on the kitchen table. I was flipping through it when I found the "Musical Instruments" page.

That's when I saw it.

"El Diablo" was a Chinese copy of a Gibson SG electric guitar. It had accentuated double-cutaways that resembled devil's horns. The body was painted in a red so vivid that it reminded me of a stab wound and branded the outline of Satan's head behind my eyelids every time that I blinked.

I spent an hour staring at it (I even took a Polaroid photograph of the page, which I carried everywhere), obsession growing inside me like a tumour as I pored over the technical specifications whilst ignoring the reality.

The price was an eye-watering £250. Even the lowest weekly payment, spread over three years was beyond my meagre budget. Asking mum was out of the question. We didn't have pot to piss in, and an electric guitar was at the bottom of the priority list.

That night I dreamt of it. We were centre-stage in a dark, stinking dive-bar, playing to a crowd of slavering, writhing and fornicating scarlet demons. El Diablo screamed out a blistering, elongated siren call laden with reverb and feedback.

As I played, the room began to shudder, the dirt floor erupting ripe mud pustules through which corpses scrabbled from their graves, stood upright, and then got their bad selves on down to the groove. El Diablo screamed louder then dive-bombed to a heavy, low-down 12-bar blues. Demons grunted like rutting pigs, shitting everywhere as the guttural power chords and driving bass line resonated deep within their bowels.

In the midst of this rancid hell-hole, one of demons separated itself from the undulating mass, turned and lumbered towards me, its breath inundating my world with unholy stench as it morphed into Keith Richards.

"You get that axe, it's gonna change your life," Keith growled. "How much of a deposit would you need to afford the payments?"

A corpse shuffled across the stage, strips of rotting material flapping and dangling from its bones, wisps of dirty grey hair creeping from beneath the rim of a filthy top hat. As it drew closer, scraps of desiccated facial muscle twitched in an obscene representation of a grin as the corpse laid its bony hand on my shoulder.

"Today is Friday," it hoarsed. "People pay their bills on Friday."

I erupted from the nightmare, my pyjamas wringing with sweat, my heart thumping as I switched on the light and waited for the images to fade.

The catalogue was on the floor where I'd left it. The photograph of El Diablo wiggling her curves at me, looking every bit as seductive as a Playboy Centrefold.

At the back of the catalogue was about ten pages of small print. I speed-read through to the payment terms and calculated that a 20% deposit would halve the weekly payments over three years. Putting El Diablo well within my limited means.

All I had to do was find fifty pounds.

It was dark when my alarm went off, and cold when I slipped out of bed. Outside, the clear sky glistened with stars, the ground with frost and icy treachery.

I was halfway along my paper round when from behind I heard the familiar clinking bottles and low whirring electric hum of Sid Davies' milk float.

Sid gave a cheery wave as he drove past and then steered across the road to stop outside a block of flats.

I watched him step out of the cab, and reach for a crate of milk bottles.

I watched him heft the crate onto his shoulder, and then turn towards the flats.

I watched him take three steps, and then his feet shot from under him.

I saw his head hit the pavement, heard his skull crack through the crash of breaking glass.

When I reached him, Sid wasn't moving. Blood poured from his ears, running along the camber of the pavement, mixing with spilt milk to create a grotesque strawberry milkshake in the gutter.

I remembered my brother telling me that if someone is bleeding from the ears, then it's not a good sign.

I knelt down and felt Sid's neck for a pulse like my brother had shown me.

Nothing.

I grabbed his wrist.

Nothing.

Sid always wore a battered leather satchel on a thin strap slung over his left shoulder. The satchel lay to one side, the flap was open and in the pool of sodium light I could see banknotes inside. Lots of banknotes.

"It's Friday. Everyone pays their bills on Friday."

"You get that axe, it's gonna change your life."

I looked up and down the street. It was still early, still no sign of any movement. No lights coming on. No curtains twitching. No one around.

I looked back at Sid. Checked his pulse again.

Nothing.

My heart pounded as I slipped my hand inside the satchel, grabbed fistfuls of notes and stuffed them frantically into my paper sack.

"Whu...whu...whu..."

I stifled a scream as a hand grabbed my wrist. Sid was awake, gripping my arm, his cheeks puffing and deflating as he blew strange words into the cold morning air.

I leaned over him. "Can you hear me, Sid?"

"Whu...whu...whu..."

"Do you know who I am, Sid?"

"Whu...whu...whu..."

His left foot began to quiver, and then shudder violently.

"Sid?"

By now his head lay in a pool of blood, his eyes staring wildly. I pried his fingers from my wrist.

"Do you know where you are, Sid?"

"Whu...whu...whu..."

I looked around. Still no sign of anyone.

El Diablo flashed into my vision. Its body pulsing like arterial blood.

"You get that axe, it's gonna change your life."

I took a deep breath, grabbed Sid's head in both hands, lifted it and then hammered it onto the pavement.

I felt something give, like the shattering of an eggshell.

"Whuwhuwhuwhu."

Sid's breathing became ragged.

I lifted his head again. This time I put the weight of my body behind it, smashing it down with all the force I could muster. Again and again and again.

Crack.

Crack.

Crack.

Sid's eyeballs rolled upwards, he gave a final clattering gasp, and then fell silent.

I smashed his head once more, saw something ooze from the back of his skull.

By now I was panting, my arms aching.

I stood up and looked around again. Still nobody about.

I stepped over Sid's body and carried on with my paper round, pulling banknotes out of my sack and stuffing them into my pockets.

Nobody saw me walking away.

Back at home, I laid the cash out on my bed.

One hundred and twenty five pounds.

Fast Forward to 1975.

By now I was getting pretty tasty. I was still underweight, still stammering, still short-sighted, and still ginger. But I could play the guitar just like ringing a bell.

Hours and hours of finger-shredding practice was finally beginning to pay off. I could play pretty much anything, any style. I had inherited my brother's record collection and developed a preference for early electric blues, and everything by the Rolling Stones up to Exile on Main St. (the last album he bought before the IRA blew him up).

The bullying had lessened somewhat. Encounters were fewer, but no less violent. Going out was safer, but the effects lingered on and my mind was still feeding me sinister thoughts.

El Diablo was my comfort blanket, soaking up my anger, calming my fears and converting my bleak thoughts into sweet tones. Whatever mood I was in, she made me sound good, and when I thought the voices in my head weren't listening, I would daydream of a playing in a band.

The Turtle Doves were formed at my school in your standard rock group formation: lead singer, two guitarists, bassist and drummer.

Mick Taylor, the lead singer was a tall, skinny narcissist who thought he was Mick Jagger. He really wasn't.

Dave Scott was the original lead guitarist. The very same spiteful, loudmouth bastard who made my formative years a living hell.

Rhythm guitarist was Alex Scott, Dave's twin brother and partner in crime.

Bassist was Jimmy Morton. Dedicated to music. Later on, Jimmy co-wrote all the songs with me.

The drummer was Tom Cornwell. Legend.

I'd watched them practice a few times at school, and noticed that cracks were beginning to appear. Jimmy wanted the band to record original material (he was a prolific songwriter), whereas Dave and Alex insisted on playing covers because they couldn't be arsed to put in the work to create something new. No one else in the band could write music and so Jimmy was outvoted every time. After one particularly memorable argument, the practice session ended with the Scott brothers storming off.

I walked out of school that afternoon to find them leaning against a wall, passing a fag back and forth. Dave's face twisted into a sneer.

"What are you looking at, you little cunt?"

"Nothing," I said.

I didn't see the first punch, just felt the explosion on my face and the familiar taste of blood in my mouth. The second punch put me on the floor, after that, all I could do was curl up tight and try and protect my head against the volley of kicks from Dave and his bastard brother.

I heard shouting, and then a scuffle, and then the kicking stopped and I was being lifted to my feet.

"Four-eyed ginger twat." The Scott brothers laughed as they swaggered away.

"Are you alright?" Jimmy looked genuinely concerned.

I sniffed back tears. "I th-think so."

"Pair of wankers," said Jimmy.

He stepped back. "I saw you watching us practice," he said. "You like music?"

I nodded. "I p-play guitar," I said.

I showed him the latest Polaroid of El Diablo.

"Nice," said Jimmy. "Listen. We're playing at the Rose and Lion on Saturday, why don't you come along? I'll make sure those two won't bother you. Maybe we can hear you play?"

"M-maybe," I said.

"See you on Saturday, then." Jimmy turned and walked away.

When he'd gone I stared for a long time at the picture.

By now the Polaroid was about six months old, the glossy paper well-worn and creased, the image beginning to fade. But as I stared at the picture the colour of El Diablo seemed to become more vivid.

"Burning like the flames of hell."

The voice made me jump. Its sinister tone suggesting another kicking was inbound, but when I looked around there was no one there.

The Rose and Lion was a down-at-heel pub in a shabby side street that led to a small park and kids' playground.

The gig didn't go well. A burly, shaven-headed punter made his way to the stage and began to heckle Dave. At first Dave tried to ignore him, but the shaven-headed guy was relentless and seemed to know which buttons to press.

Dave stopped playing, grabbed his guitar by the neck and hit the floor swinging. Punches were traded, Dave was pulled away, and Shaven-Headed Guy was bundled out of the pub.

The next morning Jimmy turned up at my house.

"We're looking for a new guitarist," he said.

Jimmy told me that after leaving the pub, the Shaven-Headed Guy waited outside. Witnesses saw him grab Dave and frog march him into the park.

Next morning, Dave was discovered near the swings. Every single bone in his body had been systematically and expertly broken.

A couple of weeks later, on a Friday afternoon, I went to visit Dave in hospital. He was out of Intensive Care and in a room on his own. Encased in a body cast, and hanging from traction wires, he looked like a wounded marionette.

I walked up to the bed and leaned in close. The bruising on his face had ripened to a midnight blue, with patchy clouds of sickly yellow. His broken jaw was wired shut, rendering his trapped words unintelligible.

Swollen, bloodshot eyes stared back at me, first with anger, then uncertainty, and then widening in fear as I licked his face, dragging my tongue from his chin to his forehead.

I leaned closer, to whisper in his ear.

"Burn in hell, you piece of shit."

I grabbed a pillow from an armchair next to the bed, placed it over Dave's face and pushed down hard.

It was over in seconds. The bed shook violently at first, and then calmed, and then silence.

I looked up at the sound of a scratch-flare, and the smell of burning tobacco.

Sid, the milkman, stood in the corner of the room, dragging on a Woodbine. His pallid, death-mask creased into a grin as smoke poured from his nostrils and mouth.

"It's Friday," he said. "People pay their bills on Friday."

Sid winked at me. "When they lifted me up," he said. "My brains fell out of the back of my head. Have a look."

He turned around. Jagged edges of skull framed a gaping hole in the back of his head, like a window pane after a brick has gone through it.

Sid turned to face me, and then nodded at Dave's body. "He's on his way. Probably burning as we speak."

His cheeks hollowed as he drew on the Woodbine. "You better go," he said.

I put the pillow back on the chair. When I looked up, Sid was gone.

I took a moment to stroke Dave's head, felt myself smile as I whispered, "Fuck you," and then I walked out of the room.

I joined the band. Jimmy and I began writing together, and gradually we built up a decent repertoire of hard-driving songs.

Without his thug twin for back up, Alex left me alone. But he still hated my guts, and I his. I bided my time.

12days Of Christmas:2017

In 1976, Malcom Maclaren's Monkees hit the UK like a lightning bolt, sparking a wildfire that swept across the country.

By 1977 our back catalogue captured the zeitgeist perfectly and we were soon compared with The Clash and The Stranglers.

Our name began to spread. A demo tape played by John Peel begat a local radio interview, which begat more gigs, which begat an offer of a deal with an up and coming indie record company, which begat a hit single, which begat another one, and another one.

We did Top of The Pops three times, became regulars on the John Peel show, and even supported the Rolling Stones for one show (John Lee Hooker was ill and we happened to be the only band in town. But still...).

After the gig, Keith Richards asked if he could play my guitar. When he picked up El Diablo, he looked at me sideways, and then winked knowingly as he played the opening riff to Sympathy for the Devil.

Later, Keith posed for a picture with me. Later still, his dealer introduced me to heroin.

We made it onto the covers of New Musical Express, Melody Maker and Smash Hits.

All through this El Diablo never left my side, and never let me down. She became my trademark, and part of music lore. I made sure she was on every album cover, picture disc and concert poster.

Gibson got to hear of it and offered to give me a real SG, provided that I agree to get rid of El Diablo. I declined, which sent Alex over the top in a thermonuclear drunken hissy fit.

"Are you fucking mad?" He screamed. "The biggest guitar company in the world have offered to give you one of their guitars, and you'd rather play that cheap piece of shit?" His foot lashed out, kicking El Diablo from her stand

Even though I'd killed two people, Alex Scott was the first and last person that I ever punched. Drawing on a lifetime of experience, I knew exactly where to hit him. The first punch broke his nose, the second his cheekbone, and the third and fourth resulted later in an eye-watering bill for cosmetic dentistry.

That was in the Green Room of The Old Grey Whistle Test, which explains why Alex didn't appear that night.

A week later, a couple of days before Christmas, we played in Belfast.

12days Of Christmas:2017

I hadn't seen Alex since I smacked him. He flew to Belfast on his own, joining us for the sound check before the gig.

I felt nervous at being there. This was the height of The Troubles and you could feel the tension in the venue. But we played a storm, the crowd roared their approval at every song. Half way through the set, Mick was introducing the band when Alex stalked across the stage, grabbed the microphone and pointed to me.

"And this little shit is our lead guitarist. The IRA blew up his brother, if any of you are in tonight I'll buy you a drink."

El Diablo buzzed in my hand. Burned behind my eyelids.

Half the crowd cheered, the other half booed. And then it kicked off. We ducked as a hail of bottles and broken seats clattered onto the stage.

Mick froze. I didn't blame him.

Jimmy came across to me. "We've got to do something," he yelled. "This is like the Stones at fucking Altamont."

I played a familiar riff. Jimmy nodded, patted me on the shoulder, and then looked at Tom.

"Stiff Little Fingers," he shouted.

Tom nodded. Mick looked petrified. "I don't know any," he said.

Jimmy shrugged. "I fucking do." He stepped forward to his mic, "1-2-3-4...!"

I played the riff again, and the crowd roared as we thundered through a monster version of "Alternative Ulster".

When we finished, the house lights came on and I saw the full extent of the ongoing carnage. The auditorium was a frenzied mass of vicious sectarian fighting. In the midst of the violence I saw a familiar face battling his way to the exit.

It was our last ever gig.

Backstage was chaos and we got separated in the melee. When we all made it back to the dressing room, Alex was nowhere to be seen. The unspoken assumption was that he'd made his own way to wherever he was going.

Jimmy looked at me. "What he said was out of order. Are you OK?"

I said I was fine.

El Diablo continued buzzing in my hand, and in my mind.

12days Of Christmas:2017

Alex was found three days later. He'd been shot through both knees and the back of the head. His hooded body left next to a burnt-out car on a patch of wasteland in Bandit Country.

The Turtle Doves split up after the Belfast gig, I haven't seen them since.

After that I bummed around. When a solo career didn't work out, I did some session work and got by. And then my mum died of cancer, and I lost interest in everything. I wasted every penny that I earned as my habit took hold, and my life spiraled into a nosedive towards yet another "Live Fast, Die Young" rock and roll cliché.

Looking back I've forgotten more than I can recall. Can't even remember the last time I played.

I tried to pawn El Diablo the other day. The pawnbroker laughed at me. People can smell desperation, and when you're a fallen rock star and drug addict the only place you'll find sympathy is in the dictionary, somewhere between shit and syphilis.

Most of my veins have collapsed, I'm half blind (injecting yourself through the eye will do that), my teeth are rotten and I've got ulcers all over my body. My worldly possessions are this notebook, a pen that I nicked from a betting shop, a sleeping bag and the clothes that are hanging off me.

And that fucking guitar. Immaculate as the day I bought it, while my life has turned to shit.

This morning I woke up under some bushes. At least it didn't rain. One of the newspapers I'm lying on is a couple of days old. The front page story is about a British Army patrol killed by the IRA in Londonderry. There are pictures of the victims, one of whom is Shaven-Headed Guy, AKA the late Sergeant Major Adam Lane, 2nd Battalion, The Parachute Regiment. Best friend of my late brother, and pall-bearer at his funeral.

The last time I saw him we were standing over the body of Alex Scott, Adam's Browning 9mm still smoking in my hand. Adam had broken Alex's leg so he couldn't make a run for it – he was good at breaking bones, was Adam – and then told me where to shoot him, to make it look like a hit.

Alex screamed like a baby, said he was sorry for all the times he and his brother beat me up, snot pouring down his face as he begged for mercy. I was high as a kite but I remember laughing when I blew his kneecaps out, and the stench of him shitting himself when I pushed the gun barrel against the back of his head.

12days Of Christmas:2017

After a lifetime of imagining scenarios of slow, violent revenge, I thought killing the Scott twins would make me feel better. Instead, all of my dark fantasies turned into terrifying nightmares - hideous dreams from which I wake screaming. And when I go for too long without a fix, my night terrors return as daylight hallucinations.

The gift that keeps on giving.

When I'm not high or hallucinating I think of Sid the milkman, how it felt to batter his head on the pavement, cracking it open until his brains leaked out.

Lately, I've seen him every day. Sometimes he talks to me, but mostly he stands to one side, smoking a Woodbine, smiling quietly, looking at his watch and biding his time.

I pick up the damp newspaper and read the story about the IRA bomb.

Sid's waving to me now, beckoning me towards him. I stand up, and sling El Diablo's strap over my shoulder for one last performance. The railway line's vibrating and I can hear the train a'coming.

"It's a Friday," said Sid. "Everyone pays their bills on Friday."

12days Of Christmas:2017

A Partridge In A Pear Tree
Lex H Jones

Barnabus Highmoor jabbed at the smouldering coal fire with his iron poker, furrowing his brow at the realisation that the flames were dying out. With a muttered curse he rose from his battered old armchair and walked over to the coal scuttle, emptying its contents onto the fire. The flames roared back to life with such sudden ferocity that Highmoor actually fell back into his chair. Another string of curse words burst forth. He'd become so jumpy lately, and he chided himself for it. Starting at shadows and loud noises; the stuff of childhood and malingering nonsense. Not suitable for a retired bank manager by any stretch of the imagination.

The embers danced as they rose before the flickering images cast on the red brick at the back of the fireplace. Highmoor stared at them, more captivated by their movement than he was by the book he held in his hands. If one were to ask him, he couldn't even rightly recall the title of the musty old thing. One more attempted distraction from his own thoughts, which like the fireplace, had lost their light of late. With a harrumph, he placed the book down on the side table and walked over to the window.

The garden beyond the glass was barren, its poorly-tended plants dead or overgrown with no apparent middle ground. The grass too, was in a similar shared state of being long overdue a cut, or patchy with large areas of brown earth showing through. The thick covering of frost gave the garden a more pleasant appearance that it would otherwise lack, as did the slowly-falling snow. The birdbath had frozen over, with several long thin icicles reaching down below the stone rim. Just behind that was the pear tree, its branches currently devoid of leaves or fruit.

"Damnable thing," Highmoor said as he stared at the tree, his face crumpling into a scowl.

Either the sight of the tree or the proximity to the window made Highmoor shudder, the previous warmth of the fireplace suddenly seeming a considerable distance away. He drew his purple dressing gown about himself all the closer to stave off the cold, then turned his back on the window. At this moment, as though it had been waiting for him to avert his gaze, something moved quickly through his peripheral vision. Too fast for Highmoor to properly make out anything close to a shape or colour, but far too large to be flakes of falling snow, and moving in the wrong direction to boot.

The source of the sudden motion was now sat atop the frozen birdbath, idly pecking at the ice. It was a partridge, brownish in colour with a blue-grey breast.

"You won't get any water from that today," Highmoor scoffed, hiding his moment's irrational fear beneath scorn poured onto a creature he considered lesser than himself.

The bird cocked its head to one side glancing up at the window with a look that suggested it heard Highmoor talking to it.

"Shoo, get away," he called, tapping on the glass as though the bird might understand the gesture. Sure enough, the bird flew away at the sudden sound, leaving the garden empty once more. The snow had started to settle now, the sight of which cause Highmoor to return to his seat at the fire.

Sleep was a reluctant companion these past few weeks, refusing to join him for more than an hour or so at a time each night. Perhaps it was off comforting others in-between the brief moments it might share itself with him. Barnabus Highmoor knew all about that, of course. The imagined figure of sleep would hardly be the first to treat him in such a way. Nevertheless, he closed his eyes as they grew heavier, happy to remain in his chair rather than moving to the bedroom if it this was where sleep was to be found.

A sudden flurry of sound and motion in the fireplace brought him immediately back out of the drift towards slumber. His gaze went sharply forwards to the fire, where he saw something resting on the coals there. The very same coals which still burned. Yet despite this fact, something stood there, its head tilting from one side to the next as it stared out at Highmoor. The partridge, as content and relaxed as it had been stood on the edge of the frozen bird bath.

How could it be in the flame? How could it stand, its feathers unsinged, the heat and smoke not seeming to bother it one bit? Highmoor scratched the side of his temple, the nervous itch there feeling like a tiny beak rapidly pecking at him. His confusion at the bird in the flames turned to frustration, and so Highmoor grabbed his poker and swung it in the direction of the fireplace. The bird didn't move. Highmoor rose from the chair and jabbed at the bird now; a focussed strike rather than a general movement to scare it away. The poker passed right through the bird, as though it weren't even there. He swung again, wilder this time so that he actually knocked several pieces of coal onto the floor. Dropping the poker, he frantically gathered the coal up using the scuttle and the edge of his shoe. When he went to empty it back onto the fire, the bird was gone. In point of fact, Highmoor now doubted it had been there to begin with.

"Poppycock and nonsense," he huffed, noisily replacing the coal scuttle and fire poker before retiring to his bedroom.

The following morning, Barnabus Highmoor shuffled down his creaky wooden staircase to the living room, eager to start the fire given the fresh snowfall. The garden was now a blanket of white, the only discerning features being the birdbath and the pear tree. As Highmoor made up the fire and went to light it, he saw something which he had not been expecting. Something that nobody would expect, if truth be told. Across the hearth and down onto the floor were a series of tiny black footprints. The prints of a bird that had been standing on coal dust, it appeared.

"Bloody, damned bird." Highmoor hurled the coal scuttle and then went to get dressed.

After venturing into town, he returned in the mid afternoon with a chimney sweep in tow.

"Bird's nest or something up there, has to be," Highmoor grumbled as the chimney sweep started preparing his broom.

"You might get that in summer, but if you've had the fire on there's not much chance of that, sir," the sweep replied.

"Don't argue with me, I know what I saw. A partridge came right down that chimney."

"A partridge, sir?"

"Yes, what of it?"

"Don't they nest on the ground? Why would on have a nest up a chimney?"

"I'm not a bloody bird expert, just clean the damn chimney."

"Right you are. I've got to say, this house looks familiar. Have I done a job for you before?" asked the sweep.

"You may have, yes. I like to hire people that I know will do a good job."

"There was a young woman here last time, I recall."

"My wife, yes. No longer here, I'm afraid."

"Oh, I'm very sorry. Was it the consumption? Lot of women falling to that around here."

"No, she's still alive. Well, as far as I know. She ran off with one of her lovers. I found the letters."

"That's a shame sir, sorry to hear that."

"My own fault for taking a much younger wife. I should have known." Highmoor shrugged. "Anyway, I'm going to pop the kettle on the stove if you want a hot tea when you're done clearing my chimney of birds."

That very evening, Highmoor found himself once more unable to truly absorb himself in his book, and had chosen to stand awhile at the window watching the snow on the garden. It was only a light and steady fall now, but the garden was already crisp and white from the previous day's flurries. The chimney sweep had finished his work and left that afternoon. The chimney was now the cleanest it had ever been, but this didn't remove Highmoor's frustration at the fact that nothing resembling a bird's nest had been found. No traces of feathers, no stray twigs. Nothing to suggest a bird had nested in any of the small outcrops found high up in the flume.

The sweep didn't like to say that his customer must have been imagining things, but Highmoor knew that was what he must have thought. Highmoor might think that himself, were he not so stubbornly sure of what he'd seen. Why would he hallucinate a partridge, of all things?

There was simply no sense to it. A thirsty man might see a cold glass of water before his eyes which did not truly exist, or a frozen one might see a roaring fire. But a partridge? Nobody would have reason to picture such a thing.

Shaking his head in dismay, Highmoor fumbled in his pocket and found his pipe. Tapping some tobacco into it, he struck a match and took his first puff. As he blew out the smoke, he saw a form through the rising swirls of grey. Something was hanging from the frozen branches of the pear tree. Had some bird or squirrel froze to death whilst clinging there, he wondered? The shape didn't look right for that, but he couldn't make it out through the snowfall and the frost on the window. A not-insignificant portion of his mind told Highmoor to leave it be, that whatever it was didn't matter, and that he ought to try once more to enjoy his book. The greater portion, however, was sure to override this, as that was where his curiosity resided.

Chiding himself with a great sigh, Highmoor threw on his greatcoat and boots, and ventured out into the garden. He tried to remain on the approximate location of the stone path, but it was difficult to be sure with the complete white-out covering the garden. As he got close to the tree, the object hanging from it became clearer, until it was unmistakeable. It was a healthy green pear, covered in a layer of frost.

"Impossible. Preposterous," Highmoor exclaimed, reaching up and snatching the pear from the branch. He turned it over in his hand. It wasn't a mirage, or an icicle that had fooled his eyes. It was a pear, frozen over, but real all the same. Could it have been there the day before, Highmoor wondered. Could he possibly have missed it? But no, even if it had, that makes little more sense. A pear wouldn't grow at this time of year, certainly not so healthily. A single day either way would make no difference. Highmoor pocketed the frozen fruit in his coat, and then returned to the house.

In the kitchen, Highmoor placed the pear on a chopping board with a knife, and brought it into the living room. This he placed by the fireplace to defrost, staring intently as the ice began to melt. Why he was so focussed on this pear was a mystery he couldn't really answer. Once more his mind battled with itself over the relevance, and even sanity, of what he was doing, but the curiosity won out as it always would.

Taking the now-defrosted pear upon the chopping board, Highmoor raised the knife and carefully sliced the pear in half. No sooner had he done so than a thick, dark red liquid poured out from it. Viscous crimson spilled from the hollow pear over the chopping board and down onto Highmoor's lap. It was warm, and had a metallic smell to it, like copper.

Highmoor rose from the chair and almost fell over as he looked down at his blood-soaked dressing gown. In a cry of fury and panic he took up both halves of the pear and threw them into the fireplace. With a roar, the flames took the fruit and consumed it impossibly fast. Highmoor watched it burn, the fire dancing in his eyes, and then looked at his blood-stained hands. Except, they were no longer stained. Nor was there any blood on his lap, the floor, or even the chopping board. He checked his hands, front and back, the gaps between the fingers, the tiny slivers beneath his nails. Nothing, no trace of red. Highmoor dropped to his knees and started laughing. He wasn't sure quite what else to do.

"I'm telling you Ernest, I didn't imagine it. My mind has never dreamt up anything that vivid without some liquid assistance," Highmoor assured his friend, as the two men sat facing each other at the fireplace.

"Had you eaten? Slept sufficiently?"

"Are you asking me as my friend Ernest, or the professional Doctor Pomp?"

"Both," Pomp replied with a smirk.

"Then it's true I've had trouble sleeping. But consider it for a moment, Ernest. How much sleep would a man need to be lacking before he'd start to hallucinate such things? You're talking about extreme exhaustion, not a few hours of tossing and turning."

"You've also got to take trauma into account, Barnabus," Ernest remarked.

"Trauma." Highmoor repeated the word with such scorn that he might as well have been spitting it out.

"Your wife left you for some young buck. A wife whose affections you'd always doubted. Her actions only served to confirm what you'd long believed, thereby justifying your years of anxiety about it. A man doesn't easily get past such things in his own heart and mind."

"That was a year ago. She left on Christmas day, in fact. The first day of Christmas, if you follow that tradition. Meaning I spent the next eleven in misery and isolation."

"Exactly. This time of year is traumatic to you. And Christmas is only a few days away now. It makes sense that the grim associations for you would come back."

"I thought you were a doctor of the body, not the mind," Highmoor scoffed.

"The two are more closely linked than most think," Pomp corrected him. "We can stress ourselves into illness, after all."

"I'm not ill."

"So what is your suggested alternative then? Ghosts? Apparitions? Why would you be haunted by such things, if we assume they exist?"

"I didn't say I had any answers, I just wanted to share with you what I saw."

"Why don't you spend Christmas with my family and I? It'll give you something to look forward to, and more importantly get you out of this house."

"No," Highmoor replied with a firm shake of his head.

"Why on earth not? I know my wife isn't the greatest roaster of goose, but you could do far worse."

"It's nothing to do with your wife's cooking and you know it. I just think it's important that I spend my first Christmas alone here. This is my house, my home. It needs to feel as such, even at this difficult time of year. I can't simply run away from it, hide amongst the company of friends and then return afterwards. I need to stand my ground, at least for this first year. And if it's thoroughly miserable then from next year onwards, if the invitation still stands, then I shall partake of the season with you and yours."

"I can't argue with your resolve. And I do understand. Just don't spend Christmas day chasing imaginary birds around your house," Pomp teased.

"If there are none to chase then I shan't," Highmoor replied, rising from his chair and moving over to the window. He wiped the fog from the glass with his shirt sleeve, the inside of the house being that much warmer than without. The clearing of the glass meant the pear tree was now in full view before him. "I've come to hate that tree," he remarked under his breath.

"Cut it down then," Pomp replied, coming to stand at Highmoor's side and placing a reassuring hand on his shoulder.

"I could, you know. It was her that wanted it there."

"Then be rid of it, my friend. Consider that medical advice."

"I shall. I'll get my axe, and…" Highmoor stopped as he caught sight of something that was not there before. Something hanging from one of the branches of the tree. "There! Do you see that?"

"See what?"

"There's a new pear on the tree!"

"I can't see any pear, Barnabus. That tree is dead for the winter."

"Look! Look there, on the right!"

"Barnabus, I'm going to write you a prescription for some laudanum to help you sleep," Pomp said with a sigh, taking his prescription pad from his pocket. "But you must make sure that you eat before you take it."

"Thank you," Highmoor conceded.

Doctor Pomp stayed for one more brandy and then put on his overcoat and said his goodbyes. He wasn't sure that he'd see his friend again before Christmas day, and so the compliments of the season were expressed before he left. Alone once more, Highmoor immediately put on his coat and boots and took an axe from the storage cupboard. He'd bought the thing years ago and never once used it, but it was finally about to earn its keep.

The axe gripped firmly in his gloved hands, he went out into the garden, trudging through the snow which had only deepened from the night before. The glistening pear he'd seen from the window still hung from the otherwise barren branch, but he ignored it and swung his axe straight at the trunk. After several strikes, his axe lodged itself in the wood, requiring him to place a foot on the tree and leverage the blade back out. He heaved three times, and on the third the axe came loose, sending him toppling backwards to the ground. From the tree there came a creaking sound, and Highmoor watched as a vertical crack split the tree open from the base where he had been hacking, right up to the top from which the branches extended.

Highmoor expected the crack to cause the tree to fall into two halves, but it remained standing. The split went deep, but not deep enough to cause it any real structural damage, it seemed. Using the axe as a rest, he pushed himself back up onto his feet and dusted the worst of the snow from his coat. He felt damp and cold now, but it wouldn't deter his work. The tree had proven more resilient than he expected, but that was no reason to give up. His resolve regained, Highmoor gripped the axe once more and approached the tree. It was only when he got closer, that he dropped the axe in shock.

Inside the crack, nestled all the way up the centre of the tree, were the chalk-white bone segments of a human spine. Surrounding these were pulsing red and purple veins, a circulatory system of some kind. More horrifying than either of those, was what lay further up the tree. A heart. Dark red, beating loud and powerful. The sight of the tree's impossible innards made bile rise up in his throat, and yet he remained rooted to the spot.

He was only shaken out of his frozen fear by the call of a bird at the top of the tree. Glancing sharply to the right he saw the partridge, sat atop the very branch from which hung the frozen pear. Highmoor watched in horror as the partridge pecked at the fruit, the tiny hole it created immediately running with thick red blood.

"No!" he screamed, turning and falling over his feet, stumbling repeatedly as he dashed back into the relative safety and sanity of his house.

To say that Barnabus Highmoor spent the remainder of the day drinking wouldn't be an untruth. In point of fact he did little else. He'd locked the doors and checked them twice, and even closed the curtains over the window which gave the view of the garden. He didn't want to see the tree, he daren't. Nothing good could come from seeing it again. If the unnatural innards of the thing were still there, this would only further his panic. If they had gone, this would strengthen the suggestion that he might be seriously ill in the head. Ernest hadn't said it in so many words, but what was what he thought. Highmoor was sure of it. Better to shut the thing out and banish the sight of it. Let thoughts of it be lost in a drunken haze.

Highmoor staggered about the house with his second bottle of brandy clutched in his hand. His feet took him unsteadily from one room to the next, ending in the guest bedroom which had been used for the past year to haphazardly store his wife's clothes and belongings. Apart from the tree, all evidence that she had once resided here was now heaped in dust-covered piles in that room. He hadn't been in the guest room since the last personal belonging of Ida's had been tossed in there and the door closed behind it, yet his drunken mind now led him there with little hesitation.

Securing his balance with a shaky hand on the foot of the bed, Highmoor glanced around the room. Atop the nearest pile of discarded clothes was a photograph he'd paid for, showing his young wife only scant days after their wedding. He had paid for the photograph himself but had wanted only Ida to pose for it. He disliked photographs of them together, her youth and beauty alongside his age and weariness only being exaggerated further when captured forever in a still image. He lifted the picture by its bronze frame and blew the dust from it, a small spider retreating around the top right corner and hiding under the back of the frame.

"Ida...my Ida," he sobbed, tracing his fingertips over her perfect features on the photograph. He sniffled and then wiped his nose on his sleeve. His demeanour changed now to anger, his face furrowed in a frown. "This is you, isn't it? I should have known. You always had to torment me. You thrived on it, fed on it like some parasitic beast, draining the joy from me. You couldn't just let me be at peace, could you?"

Highmoor tossed the picture to the floor, the glass breaking and several shards falling away. The photograph lay face-up on the ground, continuing to stare up at him as his angry tears fell towards it.

"It was your own fault, Ida. All I ever did was love you, and what was your response? To gallivant around with your lovers, one after the other. Taunting me, humiliating me. Many said the age gap was too big. Ten years is nothing, it's true; a woman finds her adult mind many years before a man does, so a decade or so works in the man's favour. But thirty years? Perhaps that was too much. But you needn't have accepted my offer of courtship, or later of marriage. You could have declined, Ida, rather than accept and then bring me so low! You cannot blame me for what I did. You can't. I wasn't going to let you leave with him, what dignity did that afford me? Had I not suffered enough?"

The picture remained motionless, but the eyes now took on a bloodshot quality. The red in them grew darker, thicker, until a steady stream of blood now ran down the photograph like crimson tears. Highmoor lifted the picture and looked at it more closely, wanting to be sure of what he was seeing. Sure enough the blood now pooled at the base of the picture frame, beginning now to spill out and drip down onto the floor.

"You're at rest now! Why can't you leave me be? Let me have some peace!" he yelled, tossing the picture across the room.

No sooner had he done so than the room seemed to echo with the sound of a woman sobbing. It came from above him, below, behind and directly in front. From every inch of that room, the same room which housed all that had been Ida's in life. He covered his ears with his hands and screamed to drown out the noise, finally finding his feet and running from the guest room, slamming and locking the door behind him.

Mr Barnabus Highmoor spent his first Christmas Eve as a secret widower sat alone by his fireplace, a decanter close by to constantly refill the tumbler in his hand. There was no wreath, no ivy around the hearth, no candles lit in celebration of the season. Ida had been one for partaking in all of that, and he had no wish to do anything that might encourage the calling up of her spirit. There had been quite enough of that already, as far as he was concerned. Tonight was to be spent in silence, and rest. Or such was his plan, anyway, but the fates often decide that the plans of men, great or small, will not come to pass.

The gas lamps were lit all through the house, everywhere except the guest room which remained locked. The darkness had taken on a frightening quality of late, and he did not wish to be alone in it. Not during this night, above all others. The last night she drew breath before his tightening grasp took it from her pale throat forever. When he allowed his thoughts to wander to that night, he questioned himself about whether he regretted it. Those who knew him were all aware of her affairs, and her plans to leave him, so her sudden disappearance had brought no suspicion on Highmoor whatsoever. It was hardly as though her waiting lover could contact the police and alert them that she had never appeared on his doorstep as they had planned. He must have surely assumed that she had opted to remain in her marriage and cease their contact.

With the threat of the law removed, all that really remained to torture Highmoor about the matter was his own conscience, and that had always been strangely light about the matter. Perhaps it was the accumulation of her harsh words and loveless actions. Humiliation upon humiliation ending with a moment's righteous fury. Others would not see it this way, of course, even if they understood Highmoor's anger. But his own mind was settled on the matter, and not the slightest bit troubled by it. At least, it had been until the first night he'd witnessed the partridge sitting in the pear tree. If the hallucinations were truly the product of his own nagging morality, why wait close to a year in which to trouble him? He couldn't reconcile this at all, and yet he still refused to outright accept the existence of ghosts. To think too strongly on the matter led to greater anxiety, so a better option seemed to be to let his mind sink into a drunken stupor for the remainder of the season.

Highmoor was happily doing just that when he heard a creaking from the upper hallway. A chill travelled the length of his spine, causing him to dig his nails into the brown leather of his armchair. Another creak, closer to the top of the stairs this time, as though someone were walking along it. The layout of Highmoor's house was such that one had to open a door at the base of the stairs to then enter the living room. This door lay behind where Highmoor currently sat, and was visible to the right side of his peripheral vision. The same door was also currently closed, in his desire to maintain the heat and light of the room. The chill down his spine changed to a cold sweat at the sight of the door creaking open behind him, slowly but deliberately. Not an act of old hinges or a stubborn draft.

Highmoor closed his eyes, not wanting to risk the imagined sight of a rotting corpse standing in the doorway behind him. A corpse dressed in the same clothes it had worn the night it had planned to leave him. His eyes closed as tightly as they could be, his teeth grinding together, the room fell silent. This silence was more chilling to him than the creaking floorboards had been a moment ago. Whatever had stood in the doorway now whispered his name. It felt as though it came from lips that were right next to his ear, bringing with it an icy cold breath that made him whimper.

Finally the tension in his body proved too great, and he sprang to his feet, grabbing the iron poker as he did so. Spinning around so that the fireplace was now behind him, Highmoor gripped the makeshift weapon and stood ready to face what haunted him. Of course, there was nothing there. The door to the staircase and hallway was also closed, as he had left it. He smirked, the unneeded adrenaline surging through him making him feel somewhere between euphoric and exhausted. He wanted to laugh, and felt as though he just might. But then the silence was broken once more by a new sound.

Tiny footsteps walked along the floor, almost too quiet to perceive above the crackle of the fireplace. He looked around for the source of the sound, but all he saw were a line of tiny black footprints along the floor, starting at the hearth. The bird again. That damnable partridge. Highmoor swung his poker wildly, as though the bird were invisible and yet might still be struck. The poker made contact with nothing save a few ornaments atop the fireplace, which duly broke as they greeted the floor. He chided himself and immediately stooped to pick up the remains. As he did so, the floorboard beneath his hand buckles and rose as though something was pressing beneath it.

He staggered back and fell into his armchair, helpless to do anything but watch as dark root of a tree pushed its way from beneath his floorboards and moved across the floor towards him like a snake. Others joined it as they uprooted other parts of the floor, all making their way slowly in the direction of the seated Highmoor. Overcoming his desire to remain fixed to the spot once more, he jabbed the closest of the snaking roots with the poker, pinning it to the floor. He then grabbed the coal scuttle and filled it with hot coals from the fire, and ran out of the house, not even bothering to put on his coat or boots.

The garden path was covered in fresh snow, and Highmoor's house slippers were hardly the safest footwear to navigate it. Nevertheless, he made it the length of the garden without slipping, standing before the pear tree with his scuttle of hot coals. As he gazed upwards, the tree was now laden with frozen pears. The crack he had caused was still there, the pulsing heart clearly visible at the top along with the chalky spine that ran down the centre and the veins that surrounded it.

Good, he thought. This only confirmed its realness. The handle of his axe stuck out from the snow where he had discarded it, and with his free hand Highmoor now took this in his grasp.

"Get back where you belong!" he screamed, emptying the hot coal scuttle into the crack of the tree.

The trunk caught fire instantly, far faster than should have been logical, as had the pear when he had tossed it to the flames. The pear tree seemed to writhe like a living thing, its branches flailing like the limbs of an octopus. The dangling pears started to drip with blood as the fire removed their covering of frost, forming a pool of blood that encircled the burning tree. Highmoor now discarded the empty coal scuttle and took the axe in both hands, then began swinging it furiously at the tree. Each impact caused a burst of blood to spray his face, but despite this and the heat, he continued. He would not rest until he was done.

Several of the burning branches leaned downwards and reached for Highmoor, forming crude hands with too many fingers. He ignored this, as he also ignored the way in which the blackened wood above the pulsing heart seemed to now form the face of his dead wife. He closed his eyes to it and kept on hacking, roaring in pain and desperation as the flames spread across his arms and back.

12days Of Christmas:2017

The policemen who arrived the following morning were not happy at having to come out to such a grim sight on Christmas morning, but they did their duty all the same. Barnabus Highmoor's neighbours had been away with family for most of Christmas Eve, arriving back early morning in time to see the aftermath of his actions. The police were promptly alerted, and arrived as soon as they were able. What they found was the charred remains of a tree that had been evidently set alight and then hacked haphazardly with no rhyme or reason. If one were aiming to simply cut down the tree, the strikes would be focussed repeatedly at the trunk, and yet the various axe wounds all about the tree indicated nothing close to this.

Whether it was the fire or the hacking of the axe, a combination of both or something else entirely, the police could not say, but whatever the reason it was the case that the tree was now completely uprooted and lying flat on the garden in a pile of ash and snow. Its blackened roots pointed towards the house like a grasping hand. More disturbing than any of this, however, was the discovery of the two corpses that accompanied the tree. One was a blackened husk clutching an axe, several tree branches surrounding it as though it had been caught in their grasp before it died. The second corpse had evidently been buried beneath the tree itself, uprooted now by its falling. This corpse was smaller, clearly female. It was wearing a coat and dress and buried next to a suitcase full of clothes, money and travelling papers.

Bonus Material

12days Of Christmas:2017

12days Of Christmas:2017

The Incredible True Story of Red Sleigh Down (Santa's Stripy 'Oss)

Ian Henery

For 6 year old Grace

You've heard the tales of Christmas past,
The ones of Santa on Christmas Eve?
Traversing the airy halls of Heavens vast
For good children, who believe
In angels, Mary. Joseph, Jesus' birth,
Peace and goodwill to everyone on Earth?

St. Nicholas, Santa Claus, its the same:
Bewhiskered, jolly and in boots -
Father Christmas! Its just a name
For the Big Guy in a red suit.
Its the one Santa, don't you know,

12days Of Christmas:2017

He comes even if there's no snow.

Magic drifts through the December air,
Wide-eyed children look to the sky;
A simple truth, nothing can compare,
At Christmas, reindeer can fly!
Children's' dreams give reindeer wings,
Believing the magic Christmas brings.

Glimpsed between clouds, a vision in moonlight,
Santa's reindeers pulling his sleigh;
Lovely Christmas presents to bring delight
In stockings, beneath trees on Christmas Day
To awaken, stretching and yawning,
Finding presents on Christmas morning.

Is this the greatest tale ever told?
Nine reindeers pulling one sleigh,
A legend spun from sagas old,
Delivering presents before break of day?
Joy to every child in every street,
The mystery of Christmas now complete?

12days Of Christmas:2017

Santa - its the same every year,
Led by Rudolph with his nose so bright:
A sleigh of presents, pulled b y reindeer,
Rudolph guiding them through the night;
More rapid than eagles, they flew,
Laden with gifts and Santa too.

He called them all by name - Vixen,
Rudolph, Dasher, Comet and Dancer;
On, Cupid, on Doner and Blitzen
And not forgetting faithful Prancer!
"Dash away, dash away, dash away all!
Tops of chimneys and over the walls!"

Christmas, Afghanistan, peace for a while:
Presents, regardless of colour or creed;
Santa shot down by a rogue missile,
Delivering gifts to children in need.
A UFO, a fat man with a beard,
And not a new weapon to be feared.

12days Of Christmas:2017

In Afghanistan, shot down, they died,
A vacancy for Santa at the North Pole;
The world stood aghast and angels cried,
There was nobody else to play this role.
RED SLEIGH Down! Santa and reindeer no more,
Just further statistics in the Afghan War.

Shot down, friendly fire in Afghanistan,
Delivering presents to girls and boys
And erased by people who don't understand
Unconditional love and simple joy.
Not all bad guys are fat with beards,
Spreading peace isn't subversive or weird

"RED SLEIGH DOWN. Its Advent. Who can help us?",
Cried the beleaguered United Nations
"Its nearly Christmas, the birth of Jesus;
Hope is lost in war's devastation,
Charity is lost in global marketing:
Where is the happiness in anything?"

12days Of Christmas:2017

Countdown to Christmas and all was bleak;
This sad, worn-out world held its breath:
Angels sobbed, shops shut, apathy peaked,
Nothing mattered anymore, the world was bereft
At winter-time, skies were cold and drear,
No glory shining at the end of the year.

In Walsall, England, an honest young chap,
Heard the calling and the Heaven-sent decree:
The path of destiny lay in his lap -
Santa's 's from Walsall in the Black Country!
I've seen Jesus in a stained-glass hue
And I'll get me an animal from Dudley Zoo!"

"Alroight, maete, how am yer, what yow after?
Reindeer all gun, yow can 'ave a zebra;
Peace, goodwill and festive lofter?
A zebra, a stripy 'oss called Debra."
"Take thee stripy 'oss with gud reason:
Save Christmas and the festive season".

Magic sprinkled on the zebra, the stripy 'oss,

12days Of Christmas:2017

Wondering why Christmas always seemed hard;
Helping to save Christmas when all was lost,
Never having seen zebras on Christmas cards.
Absent, too, in scenes of the Nativity
And decorations on a Christmas tree.

Our hero, the brave Black Country lad,
Jumped on the sleigh, to Debra a whistle,
Time to warm hearts that've turned sad
And away they flew like down from a thistle:
"Dash away, dash away, dash away, Debra!
On, stripy 'oss, on Christmas Zebra!"

RED SLEIGH DOWN! "Can Walsall's Santa do it?
The question surely must be asked;
Travelling faster than a bullet,
Is this Santa up to the task?
Come blizzard, snow, ice or rime,
To gladden hearts at Christmas time.

"Dash away, dash away, dash away, Debra!"
Eyes black as sloes, nostrils open wide;

12days Of Christmas:2017

"On, stripy 'oss, on Christmas Zebra!"
Circumferencing Earth's lands and tides,
A Walsall chap celebrating Jesus' birth,
The only hope left on this troubled earth.

The tale is complete, the tale is told,
At Christmas, Santa's still coming to town;
Festive traditions saved by a Walsall lad bold,
The incredible true story of Red Sleigh Down
And how it was saved by a loyal zebra,
Out of Dudley Zoo, a stripy 'oss called Debra.

Ian Henery
www.ianhenerypoet.com

12days Of Christmas:2017

Author Biographies

DAVID COURT

David Court is a short story author and novelist, whose works have appeared in over a dozen venues including Tales to Terrify, Strangely Funny, Fears Accomplice and The Voices Within. Whilst primarily a horror writer, he also writes science fiction, poetry and satire.

His writing style has been described as "Darkly cynical" and "Quirky and highly readable" and David can't bring himself to disagree with either of those statements.

Growing up in the UK in the eighties, David's earliest influences were the books of Stephen King and Clive Barker, and the films of John Carpenter and George Romero. The first wave of Video Nasties may also have had a profound effect on his psyche.

As well as writing, David works as a Software Developer and lives in Coventry with his wife, three cats and an ever-growing beard. David's wife once asked him if he'd write about how great she was. David replied that he would, because he specialized in short fiction. Despite that, they are still married.

You can find out more about David at www.davidjcourt.co.uk

MATTHEW CASH

Matthew Cash, or Matty-Bob Cash as he is known to most, was born and raised in in Suffolk; which is the setting for his debut novel Pinprick. He is compiler and editor of Death by Chocolate, a chocoholic horror anthology, and the 12Days Anthology, and has numerous releases on Kindle and several collections in paperback.

In 2016 he started his own label Burdizzo Books, with the intention of compiling and releasing charity anthologies a few times a year.

He is currently working on numerous projects, his second novel FUR will hopefully be launched at the convention.

He has always written stories since he first learnt to write and most, although not all tend to slip into the many layered murky depths of the Horror genre.
His influences ranged from when he first started reading to Present day are, to name but a small select few; Roald Dahl, James Herbert, Clive Barker, Stephen King, Stephen Laws, and more recently he enjoys Adam Nevill, F.R Tallis, Michael Bray, Gary Fry, William Meikle and Iain Rob Wright (who featured Matty-Bob in his famous A-Z of Horror title M is For Matty-Bob, plus Matthew wrote his own version of events which was included as a bonus).

He is a father of two, a husband of one and a zoo keeper of numerous fur babies.

You can find him here:
www.facebook.com/pinprickbymatthewcash

https://www.amazon.co.uk/-/e/B010MQTWKK

MARK NYE

Mark Nye is a fledgling author from Corby, UK. He lives with his ever suffering wife and three children. When he's not scribbling down insanity he works as a BUTCHMONGER [combined fishmonger and butcher]. He's had several short stories published in various anthologies in 2017. Mark is currently working in his first full length novel about bacteria from an oceanic trench.

PIPPA BAILEY

Pippa Bailey lives in rural Shropshire, England. Principally a horror writer, independent reviewer, and YouTube personality, her supernatural and sci-fi stories have featured in several anthologies, and zines.

Her debut novel LUX is due for release summer 2018.

DANI BROWN

Suitably labelled "The Queen of Filth", extremist author Dani Brown's style of dark and twisted writing and deeply disturbing stories has amassed a worrying sized cult following featuring horrifying tales such as "My Lovely Wife", "Toenails" and the hugely popular "Night of the Penguins". Merging eroticism with horror, torture and other areas that most authors wouldn't dare.

She isn't a one-trick pony. For less intense tales, the haunting "Welcome to New Edge Hill" and up-all-night-on-genetically-modified-coffee "Dark Roast" might be more up your street.

For more information visit her website http://danibrownqueenoffilth.weebly.com/

Or visit her on Facebook
www.facebook.com/danibrownbooks

MARK LENEY

Mark Leney lives in Bromley with his wife and daughter. He is the author of the first Extinction novel which details what would happen if a dinosaur apocalypse were to occur. If he has any fans he promises them that he will finish the second book eventually.

Mark has also contributed to several anthologies including the last volume of *Rejected for Content*, the first volume of *Full Moon Slaughter* and the Christmas anthology *12 Days*. Future stories will also be appearing in *Full Moon Slaughter 2*, *The ABCs of Murder* and *Super Sick*.

G. H. FINN

G. H. Finn is the pen name of someone who keeps his real identity secret to escape the eternal wrath of several of the ever vengeful, trans-paradimensional, eldritchly squamous Elder Gods. And avoid parking fines.

Having written non-fiction for many years, Finn began writing short stories in 2015. He especially enjoys mixing genres (sometimes in a blender, after beating them insensible with a cursed rolling pin) including mystery, horror, steampunk, sword-and-sorcery, dark comedy, fantasy, detective, dieselpunk, weird, supernatural, sword-and-planet, speculative, folkloric, Cthulhu mythos, sci-fi, spy-fi, satire and urban fantasy.

G. H. Finn's links:

Website: http://ghfinn.orkneymagic.com/

Twitter: @GanferHaarFinn

Facebook: https://www.facebook.com/g.h.finn/

EM DEHANEY

Em Dehaney is a mother of two, a writer of fantasy and a drinker of tea. Born in Gravesend, England, her writing is inspired by the dark and decadent history of her home town. She is made of tea, cake, blood and magic. By night she is The Black Nun, editor and whip-cracker at Burdizzo Books. By day you can always find her at http://www.emdehaney.com/ or lurking about on Facebook posting pictures of witches. https://www.facebook.com/emdehaney/

Her story 'For Those in Peril on The Sea' can be found in The Reverend Burdizzo's Hymn Book anthology and she recently had her short story 'The Mermaid's Purse' published in the Fossil Lake anthology Sharkasaurus. Available on Amazon https://www.amazon.co.uk/-/e/B01MRXV1WR

Her debut novel "The Golden Virginian', a tale of weed, water, magic and murder, is coming soon...

ANTHONY COWIN

Anthony Cowin is a speculative fiction writer published in many anthologies and magazines on both sides of the Atlantic. He's the author of The Brittle Birds, a successful chapbook from Perpetual Motion Machine Publishing. He's also finalising work on a charity anthology he's editing for a leading British small press called 'In Dog We Trust' that features BFS award winners, well known authors and a foreword by Emma Green. Anthony has recently landed his first novel length editing job for an American publisher for an upcoming writer. Regarding his own work Anthony is working on a horror novel, a near future sci-fi dystopian novel, both of which have received interest. Anthony also reviews and writes articles for Starburst Magazine and This Is Horror. You can connect on Twitter at @TonyCowin or www.anthonycowin.com.

PETER GERMANY

Peter Germany is a writer of Science Fiction and Horror from Gravesend in Kent who intends to finish a novel, one day.

He is influenced by writers like Dan Abnett, Scott Sigler, CL Raven and Joe Haldeman.

When not pretending to be normal at a day job, he is writing or dealing with a supreme being (a cat), an energetic puppy, and trying to wrangle a small flock of chickens. He also spends an unhealthy amount of time watching good and bad TV and movies.

You can find him at his blog: petergermany.com

RICHARD WALL

Born in England in 1962, Richard grew up in a small market town in rural Herefordshire before joining the Royal Navy. After 22 years in the submarine service and having travelled extensively, Richard now lives and writes in rural Worcestershire.

His first short story, "Evel Knievel and The Fat Elvis Diner" (available on Kindle), was soon followed by "Five Pairs of Shorts" a collection of ten short stories, and another short story called 'Hank Williams' Cadillac'.

Richard's stories reflect his life-long fascination with the dark underbelly of American culture; be it tales of the Wild West, the simmering menace of the Deep South, the poetry of Charles Bukowski, the writing of Langston Hughes or Andrew Vachss, or the music of Charley Patton, Son House, Johnny Cash, or Tom Waits.

A self-confessed Mississippi Delta Blues anorak, Richard embarked on a road trip from Memphis to New Orleans, where a bizarre encounter in Clarksdale, Mississippi inspired him to write his début novel, Fat Man Blues.

www.richardwall.org

LEX H JONES

12days Of Christmas:2017

Lex H Jones is a British cross-genre author, horror fan and rock music enthusiast who lives in Sheffield, North England.

He has written articles for websites the Gingernuts of Horror and the Horrifically Horrifying Horror Blog on various subjects covering books, films, videogames and music. Lex's first published novel is titled "Nick and Abe", and he also has several short horror stories published in anthologies. When not working on his own writing Lex also contributes to the proofing and editing process for other authors. His official Facebook page is: www.facebook.com/LexHJones

Amazon author page:

https://www.amazon.co.uk/Lex-H-Jones/e/B008HSH9BA

Twitter: @LexHJones

Other Releases by Matthew Cash

Novels
Virgin and the Hunter
Pinprick
Fur [coming soon]

Novellas
Ankle Biters
KrackerJack
Illness
Hell and Sebastian
Waiting for Godfrey
Deadbeard
The Cat Came Back
KrackerJack 2

Short Stories
Why Can't I Be You?
Slugs and Snails and Puppydog Tails
OldTimers
Hunt the C*nt

Anthologies Compiled and Edited By Matthew Cash
Death by Chocolate

12 Days Anthology
The Reverend Burdizzo's Hymn Book (with Em Dehaney)
Sparks [with Em Dehaney]

Anthologies Featuring Matthew Cash
Rejected For Content 3: Vicious Vengeance
JEApers Creepers
Full Moon Slaughter
Down the Rabbit Hole: Tales of Insanity

Collections
The Cash Compendium Volume 1 [coming soon]

12days Of Christmas:2017

Further Charity Anthologies From

12days Of Christmas:2017

SPARKS

This is a public service announcement on behalf of Burdizzo Books.
Ghosts in the machine?
Killer currents?
Demonic disturbances?

Then you need Sparks!

Keep your family safe from bulbs and batteries that go bump in the night by reading Sparks. 15 electrifying tales of horror, sci-fi, bizarro and fantasy. Visit post-apocalyptic nightmare worlds, listen to recordings of the dead, feel the friction of electric lady love and be struck by lightning from the past.
Plug in, turn on, tune in and get buzzed.
Sparks – it's alive!
ALL PROCEEDS GO TO RESOURCES FOR AUTISM

12days Of Christmas:2017

The Reverend Burdizzo's Hymn Book

From all over the world, from every race and nationality there are many different religions and beliefs. Hymns tell tales of myriad gods.

Angry gods hurling fire and brimstone at the disbelievers, promising eternal damnation in hellish post-life realms.

Others sing praises of ancient feet treading on freshly tilled earth, spreading happiness and love.
Reverend Burdizzo has rounded up a congregation of voices to sing to you these new hymns. Come join him in his choir and sing these new songs of praise. They will put the fear of God into you.

ALL PROCEEDS GO TO NAPAC

12Days of Christmas 2016

Last year saw the launch of Burdizzo Books 12days anthology. It began with twelve stories based on each day of the twelve days of Christmas. These are those stories in a collected separate volume. Each year we plan to rewrite these with different authors.

ALL PROCEEDS GO TO THE CYSTIC FIBROSIS TRUST

12Days of Christmas:
STOCKING FILLERS

A HORROR ANTHOLOGY OF SEASONAL AND NOT SO SEASONAL DELIGHTS.

A collection of short scary stories based or inspired by Christmas and the songs familiar with that time of the year. Featuring 'Anti-Claus', by horror legend Graham Masterton.

ALL PROCEEDS GO TO THE CYSTIC FIBROSIS TRUST.

Printed in Great Britain
by Amazon